'Unfortunate... tricks.'

'Do you?' he asked softly. 'What about this one, then?'

When he bent his dark head and caught her lips with his, Lauren was too startled to resist. Her knowledge that he always did the unexpected had failed to encompass this at all and while her mind was still reeling he cradled her fair head and deepened the kiss, his mouth moving over hers with enough force to tell her he was not in any way teasing.

Dear Reader

As the dark winter nights unfold, what better to turn to than a heart-warming Mills & Boon! As usual, we bring you a selection of books which take you all over the world, with heroines you like and heroes you would love to be with! So take a flight of fancy away from everyday life to the wonderful world of Mills & Boon—you'll be glad you did.

The Editor

Patricia Wilson was born in Yorkshire and lived there until she married and had four children. She loves travelling and has lived in Singapore, Africa and Spain. She had always wanted to be a writer but a growing family and career as a teacher left her with little time to pursue her interest. With the encouragement of her family she gave up teaching in order to concentrate on writing and her other interests of music and painting.

Recent titles by the same author:

PASSIONATE CAPTIVITY
DARK SUNLIGHT
A DANGEROUS MAGIC
A HEALING FIRE

POWERFUL STRANGER

BY

PATRICIA WILSON

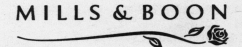

MILLS & BOON

MILLS & BOON LIMITED
ETON HOUSE, 18-24 PARADISE ROAD
RICHMOND, SURREY TW9 1SR

*First published in Great Britain 1993
by Mills & Boon Limited*

© Patricia Wilson 1993

*Australian copyright 1993
Philippine copyright 1993
This edition 1993*

ISBN 0 263 78293 X

*Set in Times Roman 10 on 11¼ pt.
01-9312-56709 C*

Made and printed in Great Britain

CHAPTER ONE

'ARE we nearly there?' Kent Redmond glanced across at Lauren as she lay back in the seat, her hair blowing in the warm, soft breeze, and she turned dark eyes on him, smiling.

'Not far. We'll be there in good time for lunch. You'll eat in a Sussex garden, the soft winds of the South Downs on you. It will get rid of a bit of that city pallor. Mummy will feed you up and look you over thoroughly.'

He glanced across at her again, his grin a bit anxious.

'I say, what do I call her?'

'Sylvia,' Lauren said promptly. 'Call her Mrs Landis and your credibility is shot to pieces. She'll feel old and you'll get the full blame.'

'It will take a while to get used to her having a different name from you,' Kent murmured. 'Without prompting I would probably call her Mrs Moore.'

'Try not to. Stick to Sylvia. It's not the wrong name that would give offence, it's the Mrs part.'

'She must be very sad really, widowed twice,' Kent offered glumly, and Lauren sat up and looked at him firmly.

'My father died when I was five years old and that's a long time ago, nineteen years to be exact. Jack died six years ago and she's recovered. At least, she seems to have. You'd better stop this Hamlet attitude or she'll think you're a pain and advise me against you.'

'Well, if she's as bright and breezy as you...'

'Where do you think I got it from?'

'I always imagined it was from a lot of money and very little work,' Kent teased, and Lauren aimed a playful blow at him.

'Settle down,' she advised severely. 'I'm presenting my future fiancé to my mother and the least she'll look for is respect. Attack me and you attack my parent. So be warned.'

She sank back in the seat again, the wind once more catching at her long hair, which glittered like silver in the sunlight. Beautiful and ash-blond, it hung in waves to her shoulders. Her face was beautiful too, delicately contoured and clear-skinned, the dark eyes and lashes a sharp contrast to her light hair.

Lauren closed her eyes against the sun, listening to the steady hum of the sports car. She imagined she was not really to be classed as a working girl. She was skilled in many things but had never really settled down to anything properly. For the past year she had been acting as a beauty consultant at one of the famous London stores but that took only part of her time.

She had quite a few pet charities but even that failed to fill her days. She was restless and she knew it, over-qualified and underworked and it was no fault of anyone but herself. At twenty-four she had never really needed to step into the world of the early commuter, the busy office and the irascible boss.

From private school to university and then to a finishing school in Switzerland, she seemed to have spent her life in studying in one way or another and it seemed to have prepared her for nothing at all. Somehow she always seemed to be waiting, making her London flat more beautiful, more expensive, stepping into the world of the rich and pampered three days a week and not earning anywhere near as much as she spent.

Kent was a rising star in one of the banks and when they married she would have to change her ways a good deal. It didn't trouble her. It would be something to hang on to, something to tie her down and quell this urge to just wander about. She had been educated for too long with no real aim in view. Money could be a curse. Kent had pointed that out frequently and he was right.

'Little Brompton?' he enquired as the car slowed down and Lauren sat up, looking round her with pleasure.

'Almost there. Take the first on the left and then straight on for a couple of miles. I'll direct you again after that. The sweet smell of the Downs, the lark on the wing, roses in the garden and crumpets for tea. I'm home,' she added quietly.

'Did you make that up?' Kent laughed.

'This very minute. Hurry along. I can't think how I ever allowed myself to be torn from this place to go to school—after school—after school.'

'Were you born here?' he asked, glancing at her entranced face. He had never quite seen Lauren like this before. Her smooth sophistication had gone, her beautiful face was softened and glowing; suddenly she was another person.

'No,' she said softly. 'I *lived* here, really lived. My mother married Jack Landis when I was seven and he bought the house. We all lived here, Mummy, Jack and me—and Ryan. We were happy, so happy.'

'Landis was rich?' Kent probed and Lauren just nodded, looking about her, only answering vaguely.

'Rich enough. He left Mummy the house and an annuity. She's comfortably off.'

'He also left you your enormous allowance.'

'No, he didn't. I didn't need anything. My allowance comes from my father, my own father.' She suddenly frowned. 'It seems to be never-ending. It just arrives.'

'Ever thought of refusing it?' Kent was watching her closely and she looked back seriously.

'Sometimes. I'm not sure what I would do, though. I don't seem to be prepared for anything. I keep putting it off. Anyway,' she sighed, 'it's mine. Once, about two years ago, I enquired. I thought it was about time I pulled my life together and I wanted to know how long this allowance would last. The bank manager was quite boot-faced. Apparently it just goes on. I came away feeling like an ungrateful wretch.'

The glow had died out of her face and Kent changed the subject speedily.

'Well, you've no worries about your mother,' he soothed. 'What about this Ryan, though? Did he get the bulk of his father's money?'

'Naturally. It was a situation that we all knew would happen one day. Ryan's uncle, Jack's brother, ran the business in the States. He was older than Jack and simply took over when Jack came to live here. Apart from a few business trips, Jack never went back to the States but it was all tied up legally. When Jack died, Ryan got his shares and when his brother died Ryan got his too. It was like a Greek tragedy. A year after Jack died, his brother was killed in a plane crash. It was the end of everything because Ryan went home, back to California. He had a multi-million-pound business to run and his trips here became few and far between.'

'So your family split up?'

'Dashed asunder. I went on learning and learning, England, Switzerland. Ryan went on making money and the golden days ended. I never see him now. The last time he came I was at school in Switzerland so I even missed that.'

'Poor little rich girl,' Kent murmured and she flashed him a look that quite silenced him. At least he had the good sense not to try goading again, either sardonically or in a kindly manner.

'Perhaps I am,' Lauren said thoughtfully after a minute. 'Spoiled little rich girl maybe. I only know I would sometimes trade it all for one more day in the past.'

'That's morbid.'

'It is.' She was smiling again, straightening up. 'Your fault, though, probing into my ancestry. Now I'll have to relax and breathe in the air again. Kindly keep silent unless you need directions.'

Kent laughed and relaxed. He had never known her like this before. Coming down here seemed to have been a mistake although they could hardly get engaged without her mother's blessing.

'We're here,' Lauren suddenly said quietly and Kent stopped the car by a white gate, a little startled at the house he could see across wide expanses of lawn. Knowing Lauren, he had expected something much more grand and although this was grand enough it was also quite modest, compared to what he had in mind.

'A sixteenth-century manor house,' Lauren pointed out, slanting him an amused look. 'Don't tell me you expected a castle?'

'I'm not sure.'

'Well, in case you're disappointed, I can tell you that Jack wanted something very English but very homely and this is it, Langbourne Manor. He bought it just before he married my mother. We all trailed down from London to see it and Ryan and I fell in love with it at first sight. We never did own the woods that stretch around but we always behaved as if we did.'

'It must have been good out here to have a ready-made playmate,' Kent mused, and Lauren burst into laughter.

'Playmate! You can't mean Ryan! He was nineteen when our parents married—very condescending. By the

time I was ten and Ryan twenty-two, he was an established tyrant.'

'Really?'

'No.' Lauren grinned and led the way to the door. 'He
pulled me out of trouble, stuck up for me and generally
ruled my life. If Ryan said no, then that's what it was—
no. He picked me up when I fell down, ordered me home
if I was out late, vetted my friends and vanquished my
enemies. He practically brought me up, when I look back
on things.'

The front door suddenly opened and Sylvia Landis
descended on them like a whirlwind. Like Lauren she
was very fair, still a beautiful woman and she gathered
Lauren close, hugging her and talking happily.

'It seems like ages! I feel as if I've been looking out
of the window since daylight. Finally, it was Olga who
saw you.'

A small dark woman came into the hall and did some
hugging of her own and then Lauren turned to Kent.

'This is my mother, and this is Olga who does just
about everything here and keeps my mother under
control.'

'How are you, Mrs Landis?' Even after all her
coaching, Kent chickened out at the last minute and
Sylvia Landis glanced at her daughter in amused
exasperation.

'Well, that puts me firmly with my generation,' she
murmured, and Lauren grinned at her cheerfully.

'I told him but I think you shocked him by appearing
like a dervish with Olga in tow.'

'Call me Sylvia,' Lauren's mother ordered with a
smile. 'You'll get used to me.'

Kent couldn't quite reckon them up. There was money
here, ease, but there was no sign of frostiness to Sylvia
Landis. Olga was looking him over carefully and he
managed a smile at her. Of the two, she was perhaps the

most daunting. She looked as if she might have once been Lauren's nanny. Lauren's mother looked a little fluffy-headed.

He relaxed. He had been dreading this ordeal. He might have known that Lauren did exactly as she pleased. This was nothing more than a courtesy visit. It was impossible to imagine Sylvia Landis forbidding any engagement and even more impossible to imagine Lauren listening to words of caution.

It was easy to talk after that and as he went to his room at the front of the house Kent felt satisfied with events. The sudden feeling he had had of being alienated from Lauren quite gone. Even though she was back here where she had obviously been happy, the same old smile had surfaced and she had slid back into her way of sophisticated chatter he knew so well.

In the kitchen, Lauren was confronting her mother.

'Well?' she prompted.

'Be specific,' Sylvia ordered, busily preparing lunch. 'You know my rule—no comment unless a definite request is made.'

'On the matter of Kent,' Lauren ordered, 'I require a comment. This is an official request.'

'He seems quite nice, dear,' Sylvia murmured.

'I don't know whether that's diplomacy or disclaiming responsibility,' Lauren complained. 'You're a cunning parent. I suppose you're hedging your bets?'

'You're twenty-four,' Sylvia pointed out, pausing in her preparations with a salad. 'Whatever we decide in life we decide by ourselves. In any case, if I say he's wonderful, you'll accuse me of going over the top. You will also ignore words of caution. I realise I can't win and act accordingly; that's what makes me a cunning parent.'

'I brought him for you to see,' Lauren stated seriously.

'An animal out of its habitat is difficult to judge,' Sylvia mused, back to her preparations. 'How long have you known him?'

'Six months, maybe a little more.'

'Then at the risk of interfering I advise caution. You can't know a person in six months, not enough to contemplate a life of marriage, not unless you're wildly in love,' she added quietly, shooting a very intent glance at Lauren.

'Wildly in love? No,' Lauren admitted honestly. 'In any case, I wouldn't recognise that state of mind if it sprang up and hit me.'

'I think you would.' Her mother went briskly past her to the fridge. 'As it obviously hasn't, you could be in for a shock. Wait, therefore.'

'I need to get my life sorted out,' Lauren muttered, almost to herself.

'And that,' Sylvia proclaimed, 'is a pretty stupid reason for marriage. It could lead to unhappiness for both of you. Wait until love hits you—the fall of fire.'

'It may not be Kent, then,' Lauren pointed out.

'Then what a lucky escape you'll both have had. In any case, how do you know? Sometimes, love just bursts into flame without warning, even with someone you think you know well.'

'It sounds like a very chancy business,' Lauren mused. Her mother had never spoken like this before. On the other hand, she had never demanded comments before and she wondered uneasily why she was doing it now. She had never had any doubts until she came back here. Perhaps, like an animal, she too had changed in her natural habitat. London seemed very far off if truth were known.

Memories lingered in this house, wonderful ghosts that teased and stood at the edge of her mind. The urge to reach out and grasp them was overwhelming, but if she did it would alter everything and she knew that instinctively. She wasn't sure if she had the courage to do that.

By lunchtime, Lauren had fought her way back to normality. During lunch, Sylvia went out to answer the phone and when she came back she was very obviously happy.

'That was Ryan,' she announced, when Lauren looked at her enquiringly. 'He just flew in.'

'And?' Lauren watched her breathlessly, a tremendous feeling of time standing still inside her and Sylvia laughed and then leaned across to hug her.

'He'll be here this evening—early!'

'Oh, bliss!' Lauren's face lit up with happiness. Here was one ghost she could safely face. 'Ryan here. I can hardly believe it. I haven't seen him for six years.'

'Well, I wrote to tell him about your forthcoming engagement so I expect he's coming to see you,' Sylvia said comfortably. 'You've managed to miss each other for long enough. Anyway, I imagine he's here on business too. He doesn't seem to get much time to himself. The last time he came he was merely stopping over on his way back from Germany. He had to go to Japan the week after that.'

Lauren was hardly listening. It was like a piece of jigsaw fitting smoothly into place because somehow nothing was real unless Ryan was there. She had forgotten over the years.

'What sort of business?' Kent asked Lauren later when they walked round the garden. 'I thought his business was in America.'

'It's pretty much all over,' Lauren confided. 'Jack and his brother inherited the whole thing from their father and they built it up to be a small giant. Ryan made it into a big giant.' She shot him a quizzical look. 'What sort of a banker are you anyway? Surely you've heard of the Landis Group?'

Kent looked stunned. Who had not? It was a huge corporation with interests in everything from microchips to building. Somehow he had not made the connection.

'I never gave much thought to the name,' he confessed. 'Somehow I...' He looked round at the peaceful garden and lovely house and shrugged his shoulders. Lauren smiled to herself.

'You mean we seem too humble to have anything to do with a multi-million-pound tycoon? We are, except that Mummy was like a mother to Ryan and he just about ruled my life for ten years. Jack sank into an English background as I told you and Ryan considered this to be his home, in spite of university and business school in America. I don't think he particularly wanted to go when duty called but he had no choice.'

'The Landis Group,' Kent mused. 'Isn't he a bit young?'

'Thirty-six. He was only twenty-nine when he took over. He was already used to flying out there to deal with things for Jack, though, and he's got the same business brain that his father and uncle had. You'll see him soon enough.'

'Maybe he'll object to the engagement,' Kent said worriedly. 'Maybe he'll want to boss you about?'

'Ryan? He's my friend,' Lauren said softly. They walked through into the orchard and she went forward as she saw the old swing. 'Ryan made this for me. I was about ten. Mummy thought it was dangerous but Ryan always got his way and I badly wanted a swing.'

'So he's the one who spoiled you,' Kent surmised, and Lauren began to swing lazily, her eyes closed against the sun.

'All the time.' She opened her eyes and smiled at him. 'Always providing that I did exactly as I was told. I haven't seen him for so long. I can hardly wait.'

Once again there was the softened expression and Kent watched her thoughtfully. Sometimes, Lauren's gloss worried him. He knew exactly where he was going and Lauren was well equipped to rise with him. The trouble was, she already had the polish that many of his superiors' wives lacked. It could lead to petty jealousies.

It was a relief to see her in this mood, her sophistication gone. Like this, tender and gentle, she was even more alluring, suddenly obviously young. He smiled and held out his hand, an unusual urge to protect her overwhelming him. Lauren rarely looked as if she needed protection. Maybe she was secretly scared of this Ryan? They would present a united front to him.

Ryan came in the late afternoon and nobody heard him arrive. They had not expected to see him so early, and, as it was, the sunlight was still strong, just beginning to edge the sky with red. The sitting-room was filled with the golden light and as Lauren sat with Kent, taking tea, Sylvia suddenly opened the door and ushered in a tall, dark-haired man who simply stood and looked at Lauren, a smile tilting his lips.

There was something about him that challenged, an indefinable air of command that brought Kent to his feet. Curious green eyes raked over him momentarily, almost making him shudder. Cat-green but definitely not any domestic cat. Kent tensed up. He was not in any way imaginative but it seemed that the jungle was suddenly around him, inexplicably menacing.

After the one all-encompassing glance, the whole of the man's attention was for Lauren. He said nothing at all, his glance never leaving her. Sylvia stood beside him smiling and Lauren too stood, slowly, as if she was in a dream.

In a way, she was. She suddenly realised that six years was a very long time. Ryan had hardened like polished steel. His peculiar green eyes were more than ever com-

manding in a tanned face. For a second she struggled
to find her childhood hero, her friend, and he wasn't
helping at all. He was a powerful man who seemed to
be light-years away from her and she felt a wave of
grief—something lost.

It was the smile that brought her to reality, that long,
tilted smile she remembered so well. It grew, touched his
eyes and the hard green changed as she remembered. It
must have been the late sunlight on his face that had
hardened him but there was still a slight feeling of awe.

'Ryan?' Lauren just stood looking at him and his head
tilted enquiringly.

'You need introductions? Perhaps Sylvia will oblige?'

'It—it's just that you look somehow different.' Lauren
felt flustered, the first time she had felt like that for years.
With Ryan there was no sophistication to hide behind.
'You're so tanned. If—if you were fair, your hair would
be bleached by the sun.'

Sylvia burst into laughter and Ryan looked at Lauren
with quizzical amusement.

'If you had any intelligence, you'd be dangerous,' he
murmured and the dark, sarcastic voice brought her back
to life.

'*Ryan*!' She raced across the room, the unexpected
worries forgotten, and two arms like iron gathered her
up as she flung herself at him and wound her arms round
his neck. He lifted her right off her feet for a second
and then slid her to the floor, his hands on her slender
shoulders as he summed her up critically.

'Let's see if I approve,' he ordered, his glance moving
over her. He smiled down at her as she stared up almost
mesmerised, drinking in the sight of him. He had always
been tall but now he seemed to tower over her and she
felt once again like a girl, back under Ryan's power. It
was a funny feeling, not altogether comfortable. It had
been a long time and she felt mournful, as if she had

lost something precious because of neglect. 'Don't burst into tears,' Ryan said wryly, looking into her eyes. 'You'll do. I can't think of any improvements I would make.'

'Still too slender,' Sylvia put in with a sigh and Ryan nodded, summing Lauren up even further.

'She always was. We never did manage to fatten her up.'

'Kindly stop talking about me as if I were the family piglet,' Lauren ordered, and Ryan laughed down at her, looking so much like himself again that Lauren's rather tight shoulders relaxed. It was all right. It really was Ryan. She suddenly smiled up at him, her expression softened, brilliant, and his eyes flared over her face.

'The family swan,' he corrected, holding her dark eyes with his.

'Oh, Ryan! It's so good to see you,' Lauren said softly and she got that old tilted smile.

'Don't speak hastily. I can't promise to keep on handing out compliments.' He looked up at Kent who still stood watching. 'So the family is expanding?' Ryan's arm came round Lauren as she turned rather guiltily to Kent, admitting that for a few moments she had quite forgotten him.

'Oh, I'm sorry. This is Kent Redmond,' she said quickly and then Kent got the full force of the probing green gaze. He came forward rather hastily to shake hands, a little blaze of annoyance flaring when Ryan Landis still held Lauren.

'I've been hearing about you all afternoon,' he offered, covering a feeling of alarm with a smile. He had rather dismissed Lauren's mother. He still found her fluffy-headed.

It seemed ridiculous now to remember that Olga had slightly worried him, ridiculous in the face of the fact that here was a real cause for alarm. He was facing power here and he knew it, cynical power, a man who would ruthlessly chop anything he disapproved of. Moving on the very edge of a circle of power himself, Kent recognised all the signs, but he had never seen anyone quite like Ryan Landis before. This man was a hard force, someone he would not care to tangle with. Just the way he stood proclaimed a physical co-ordination that was more than impressive.

'She waited until this afternoon to tell you about me?' Ryan enquired lazily.

'Lauren is rather secretive,' Kent volunteered, pleased that he could tell this man something he didn't know. There was a proprietorial air about Landis. He had only just arrived and the whole place seemed to revolve around him, Lauren too.

'Got something to hide?' Ryan tilted Lauren's chin and looked down at her wryly. She laughed up at him. She was used to this bantering and she almost had him back in his old, comfortable place.

'Honestly, you'd quite slipped my mind. It was only because Kent asked.' Ryan laughed too and Sylvia had the chance to get a word in.

'If you want to change, Ryan...?'

'I do. I've been flying for long enough. I need a shower and I need to unpack. My old room?'

'Of course.' Sylvia reached up and kissed his cheek and he smiled down at her before turning to the door.

'See you at dinner,' he warned Lauren. He nodded pleasantly at Kent and walked out. They could hear him talking to Olga in the hall and Sylvia almost danced out to join him.

'So that's the mighty Ryan,' Kent mused, looking out of the window as Lauren moved back to sit down. 'Not quite what I expected. He's not typically American.'

'Is there such a thing?' Lauren enquired. 'In any case, Ryan never was typically anything. He's cosmopolitan.'

'Like you?' Kent spun round to look at her and she laughed.

'No, not like me. I just seem to play at things. Ryan makes things happen. He's one of those peculiar people who wears authority easily. Even if I had authority, I wouldn't know what to do with it.'

'That's because you're so sweetly feminine,' Kent assured her, coming across to take her into his arms. He knew he had lost his hold on her for a while and he intended to get it back.

His lips were searching for hers when a sound at the door had them both looking up and Lauren felt very confused to see Ryan standing there, his jacket discarded, his tie askew.

'Put the car away for me, Lauren,' he asked, tossing her the keys. She caught them neatly and turned to the door.

'Don't look for slavery and boot-licking,' she warned tartly and he grinned at her as he turned away.

'That particular slavery got you started with your driving at fifteen,' he reminded her. 'Not many children are allowed to park a Porsche.'

'Did you hire a car in London?' She followed him into the old hall and he went on to the stairs without looking round.

'Hmm.'

'Are you tired, Ryan?' Lauren asked softly and he turned at the bottom of the stairs to smile at her.

'Not particularly.'

'Then why can't you park the damned car yourself?'

'Perhaps I wanted to see how sweetly you obeyed still.' He looked down at her ironically as he stood on the bottom step. 'On the other hand, a slave should be kept busy. Clearly you were about to get into mischief.'

'Ryan! I'm twenty-four and about to become engaged!' Lauren's cheeks flushed at his amused look. He
had walked in at a very inopportune moment.

'So you are, sugar. Park the car, there's a good girl.'
When she glared at him he just went on laughing and
Lauren couldn't keep a straight face. Anyway, it was
good to do things for Ryan again. She went to park the
car and inside the sitting-room Kent turned away from
his intent listening. Fitting into this family would not be
at all easy as long as Landis remained here. Fortunately
he was a big wheel and would have a very limited time
to be in England.

When Lauren came down for dinner later, everyone
else was already there, gathered in the sitting-room with
drinks. She had taken a little longer than usual because
she couldn't seem to get her mind into any comfortable
attitude. There was a feeling in the air that she had picked
up but she couldn't quite understand it.

For one thing, Kent was on edge and she knew she
had neglected him since they had arrived. Coming home
meant so much to her that she had just wanted to drink
in the atmosphere silently. Ryan's arrival had completely
thrown her off balance. He was different, but then, so
was she. Years had passed. She couldn't expect the same
old relationship.

Ryan had changed a great deal, hardened. Never a
man to be easily overlooked, he now seemed to be too
important, almost aloof in spite of his smiles. Slipping
back into their old relationship would not be easy.

Lauren fastened her hair up, a cool severe style she
used for work. It showed off her pale beauty, her superb
bone-structure, but it was a little like a disguise and she
knew it. She wore a silk dress, easy and flowing, the pale
coffee background strewn with turquoise flowers, and
as she walked into the sitting-room Kent almost caught

his breath. Tonight there was something very special about her.

Ryan looked unimpressed.

'Drink, Lauren?' He looked a bit sardonic, as if she weren't old enough, and Lauren found herself smiling secretly. Ryan had missed out too. Maybe it hadn't dawned on him that six years had passed.

'Dry sherry, please.' She walked over to Kent and wound her arm in his and he looked quite relieved. She kept close to Kent at dinner too and it brought him a little out of his shell. Lauren had never seen him subdued before, but then, she was a little subdued herself and there was no secret as to why. Ryan dominated the room even when he wasn't speaking. She tilted her head and studied him across the table. He was too powerful, quite different.

His eyes met hers and one dark brow quirked at her questioningly but she kept her thoughts to herself. There was no way Ryan was going to find out that he was worrying her. She would simply be herself.

'Do you have any staff here—er—Sylvia?' Kent suddenly asked, feeling that conversation was somewhat lagging.

'Servants? No. I couldn't do with them. We have a daily who keeps the house in order and Olga and I both like cooking.'

Olga wasn't there and Kent ventured a question.

'Has she been with you for long?'

'Always. She was with me when Lauren's father was alive and she moved down here with us. She's part of the establishment.'

'I imagined she was Lauren's nanny,' Kent ventured.

'That was me,' Ryan said sardonically. 'Lauren needed a nanny with muscle. It took all my skill to raise her.' His eyes narrowed in amusement on Lauren's flushed face. 'She's not as cool as she looks.'

He might be amused but there was something in his attitude that left Lauren feeling uneasy again.

'It's no use trying to put Kent off,' she assured him pertly. 'He knows my irritating ways.'

'All of them?' Ryan's lips quirked and Kent hastily stepped in.

'As far as I'm concerned she's perfect. We'll sort any problems out when we're married. I expect I have irritating ways too.'

It was all rather embarrassing and just a little threatening but Lauren could not quite be sure where the threat was coming from. All she did know was that Kent was bristling and Ryan was goading. It wasn't working out as she had hoped.

CHAPTER TWO

LATER Lauren found it impossible to sleep. Far from being wonderful, Ryan had upset things. All she was sure of was that he was being aloof, looking down his nose at things. Maybe he had grown too important for them after all, although he seemed still to be as close as ever with her mother.

Lauren put on her robe and went down the stairs. At least she had the house to herself. It was almost midnight and everyone else was fast asleep. It would give her the chance to roam around downstairs and breathe in the old atmosphere, because tonight she needed it. She made a drink in the kitchen and then wandered through the hall, switching off the light and going into the sitting-room.

'Come into my parlour.' The dark voice made her jump. Moonlight was flooding the room and she could just see Ryan sitting on the settee.

'Why haven't you got the lights on?' Lauren pressed a switch by the door; all the lamps came on and Ryan grunted in annoyance, covering his eyes for a second.

'I like the moonlight and I was here first.'

He was sitting with a glass of whisky, the bottle on the table beside him, and Lauren looked at him in astonishment.

'You're drinking!'

'I feel the need. Come and join me. We'll get roaring drunk and sing loudly.'

'You sound as if you're already well on the way,' Lauren pointed out primly. She walked across to get the bottle but Ryan's hand fastened round her wrist.

'Leave it! I'll choose my own poison.'

'Whisky and jet-lag. You'll be in a fine state tomorrow.'

'Don't bank on it.' He slanted her a look from beneath dark brows. 'This is my first drink. I was just settling in.'

'I'll make you some tea,' Lauren offered, suddenly alarmed, but he grimaced and let her wrist go.

'Thank you but no. With a couple of these I'll sleep.'

She didn't know what to say because this was a Ryan she didn't know at all. Walking out didn't seem like a good idea and she sat facing him, drawing the long skirts of her robe closely around her. For a minute Ryan just watched her closely until she felt like some sort of prey.

'When's the engagement?' he asked quietly.

'When we get back to London. I thought Mummy should be told first. We'll have a party to celebrate; maybe she'll come but somehow I don't think so.'

'Why not have the party here?' Ryan asked but she shook her head.

'All our friends are there. I don't know anyone here now—well, not really. I've been away too long.' She avoided his probing gaze, feeling a little lost. At one time she would have planned things with Ryan, asked his opinion.

'And what about the wedding?' he enquired.

'Oh, here of course. The village church, but we haven't set a date. Will you give me away?'

'No!' He took a drink from the glass and looked quite uninterested and Lauren looked at him mournfully.

'But why, Ryan? I thought you'd want to. I—I imagined that...'

'In the first place it's a job for your uncle Charles,' Ryan said coolly. 'He's the only uncle you've got now. In the second place, I can't guarantee that I'll even be here.'

'Not for my wedding?' She stared at him bleakly and he grunted with irritation.

'I'm busy almost all the time, Lauren. If anything comes up I have to be there. It would leave you with a problem; better to count me out.'

'I see.' Lauren looked down at her drink. It was going cold and she was even more agitated than she had been when she had got out of bed.

'I'm sure you don't see,' Ryan said harshly. 'You're not too good at working things out.'

'You don't know me any more,' Lauren pointed out hotly, hurt at this attitude. 'You haven't known me for a long time. It doesn't matter, though. When the time comes I'll contact Uncle Charles. I'm sure life will go on without your consent.' She got up to go, walking past him, but his hand shot out, capturing her wrist again and jerking her off her feet.

'Sit down, you little shrew,' he growled, pulling her down beside him. 'I suppose you've progressed in your own way.'

'I don't particularly want to sit here with a drunk,' Lauren pointed out angrily, wriggling to get free.

'I've only just started,' he assured her. 'This is my first glass; drunk comes later. Anyhow, surely this is normal for us? How many times have we sat here when everyone else was in bed, thrashing out your problems?'

'I don't have problems,' Lauren informed him. He had her pinned with one arm round her shoulders and she felt just a little like a mouse in a trap. 'It's a long time since you sorted out my problems and I object to you telling Kent that you were my nanny. You were my friend; at least, I thought so.'

'Now you doubt it? Friendship lasts a lifetime.'

'Only if you work at it.' Lauren sat up stiffly, inexplicably uneasy with him. She didn't quite know what he would do. Ryan was very different, almost verging on dangerous.

'Let's work at it. How long have you known Redmond?'

'His name is Kent,' Lauren pointed out. 'If we're trying to be friendly that's not a good way to begin.'

'Want to bet that he doesn't think of me as Landis?' Ryan asked drily. 'He never kissed my cheek. Everybody else did.'

'You're being impossible,' Lauren said hotly, spinning round to look at him.

'No more than usual.' He looked down at her intently. 'What exactly does he do at the bank? Winterbourne and Bond, isn't it?'

'You've been checking on him?' She glared at Ryan and he shook his head, looking back at her levelly.

'He told me over drinks, before you made your impressive entry. I haven't had the chance to check on him—not yet.'

'It's none of your business!'

'I can't see how you arrived at that conclusion,' he said softly. '*You* are my business, Lauren. You always were. So what does he do at the bank?'

'I'm not sure,' Lauren confessed uneasily. 'I've never really asked.'

'An astonishing lack of interest.'

'You're behaving like a headmaster,' Lauren said crossly, glaring at him again.

'The headmaster sat with his arm round you?' Ryan enquired with mocking surprise. 'You really should have told me sooner. It's all too late now. Back to Redmond.'

'He—he's working his way up. Apparently, he's got wonderful prospects.'

'Ah!' Ryan moved his arm and settled back thoughtfully, reaching for his glass. 'You're dismissed, Lauren,' he said quietly. 'Go to bed. Nowadays I drink alone.'

She sat up and looked at him in astonishment, not sure whether he was joking or not, and he never even glanced at her. He snapped his fingers and pointed to the door and she stood and glared down at him.

'You're impossible, do you know that? I could hardly wait to see you and you're quite impossible.'

'You wanted your old friend back?' He flashed her a look that she could only interpret as caustic and she flushed angrily.

'I don't want anything!'

'Then you'll not be disappointed.' He just looked away and Lauren stormed out of the room, only just stopping herself from slamming the door. She didn't know Ryan at all and the realisation devastated her.

Next morning, Lauren was up early. It was a lifelong habit when she was home. Ryan had started it, his walks with her a delight to look forward to each day, and she had never stopped, even when he finally left.

It was bright, sunny but as yet there was a slight chill in the air and in jeans and sweater she let herself out of the house and set off towards the woods. She wasn't looking forward to today really, not with Ryan there, and she wondered how long he would stay. For her it was merely a long weekend; Kent had to be back at the bank on Monday morning. She felt very mournful about Ryan, sadly let down, admitting that she wanted to get back to London before his changed attitude upset her further.

She couldn't really understand it, unless of course her first impression of him had been correct and he had hardened beyond anything she could have imagined. That was big business, the stress of it, the power of it.

Somehow, though, she had never expected him to change. She was not comfortable with him at all now.

She had wanted the old ghosts back, had wanted to cling to Ryan and just step back into the days of happiness. There was nothing to cling to. Ryan was a powerful being she didn't know at all.

'Old habits die hard, I see.' A hand grasped her arm and Lauren jumped guiltily as she looked up and found Ryan towering over her.

'I never heard you coming.' There was a certain amount of accusation in her voice and he gave her a very wry look.

'I walked on the grass. You looked so deep in thought that I wondered if you were talking to yourself. Naturally, I wanted to hear.'

'I'm surprised you can even see this morning,' Lauren said tartly, feeling her face flush. She almost *had* been talking to herself and all of it about Ryan. 'If you recall I left you clutching a whisky bottle last night.'

'Not for long. Sleep caught up with me. Where are we going?'

'I don't know where you're going but I'm going on the path through the woods and back down the drive.'

'OK. Suits me.' He released her arm and matched his steps to hers. This morning, in a thick sweater and jeans, he looked a little more like the old Ryan but Lauren was taking no chances. He hadn't been particularly nice last night and she was still smarting from it. In any case, she felt a little tongue-tied.

'How long are you staying?' It was Ryan who finally broke the silence as they walked into the woods and found the old path.

'Sunday afternoon. We have today only. Tomorrow morning Kent will start to get restless. He has to be back at the bank on Monday morning.'

'What about you?'

'I don't have to be in London until Tuesday night but of course I'll leave with Kent.' She knew her voice was stiff. She dared not relax, not when he seemed to be ready to pounce on her. If Ryan noticed he showed no sign of it.

They came to a fence and he just lifted her and dropped her lightly on the other side before vaulting over himself. He always had done that, he never even thought about it. How could he be so comfortable with things when she was on edge? Perhaps he was now too superior to care?

'What's this beauty business that Sylvia tells me about?' he enquired.

'I act as a consultant. I'm trained!' She was instantly on the defensive, knowing that she was just passing time doing what she did. She expected criticism but Ryan glanced at her curiously.

'Do I doubt it? I don't need to see your certificates.'

'I couldn't have taken the job without them,' Lauren said heatedly. 'I'm trained for a lot of things. As a matter of fact, I'm a cordon bleu cook too. I could easily run a catering business, or be one of those high-class house-keepers. I can type too *and* I'm a trained social hostess!'

'You also have an excellent appreciation of music and speak three languages. I followed your progress. Why are you getting so steamed up about it?' Ryan stopped in the middle of the path and confronted her and she didn't think it wise to duck round him and run.

'You seemed just a little sceptical. The expression was enough—"this beauty business". I imagine I'm on the defensive.'

'A pointless waste of emotion. I refuse to apologise for being male and, to a man, "this beauty business" is a normal sort of phrase. We just don't understand it.' He tilted her flushed and slightly mutinous face. 'Or are you simply looking for a fight?'

'No, well—maybe.' She suddenly relaxed, the urge to fight going. 'I suppose I feel slightly inadequate at the side of you. You're big guns. You're not playing at anything.'

'I've never had the chance,' he murmured ironically, turning back to the path as they continued the walk. 'I was catapulted into it, if you recall. Luckily, I enjoy it.'

'Do you think perhaps that power has gone to your head?' Lauren asked, wanting to shake him out of his aloof attitude. His retaliation was swift. He wound his hand in her long hair and gave a sharp tug.

'Do *you*?' he asked threateningly and she cringed closer to escape the punishment.

'Ryan! You're hurting me!'

'Am I?' He released her at once. 'I seem to have spent a good deal of time making sure you were not hurt. It's patterned in, I expect.' He sounded a bit weary and as they stepped out of the wood and on to the drive Lauren turned to him impulsively.

'Friends?' She held out her hand and he took it in his, looking down at her intently.

'I could prove to be a very awkward friend. Are you quite sure that's what you want?' Lauren just nodded, wanting him back in his rightful place, and his smile softened as he suddenly kissed her hand. 'We can try but things are not always static. Time changes everything.' They walked up the drive and he added, 'Let's celebrate the renewal of friendship. What about dinner tonight at the White House?'

'Oh, yes! It's ages since I went there, not since you took me actually.' Lauren looked up with pleasure to find the green eyes watching her closely. 'I had my first dinner-dance there too, if you recall.'

'I do recall. You took three hours to get ready.'

'It was very important to me.' She suddenly remembered something that brought a flush to her cheeks and changed the subject speedily. 'The swing is still intact. I went on it yesterday.'

They were back to the house and she darted away into the orchard, suddenly very anxious to leave Ryan for a minute and gather her composure a little. The White House had rung a very big bell in her mind and she hoped it hadn't done the same for Ryan.

'That's a very old swing.' Ryan was into the orchard swiftly but Lauren was intent on being very normal and she pushed off vigorously on the swing before he could stop her. She supposed that this action was not very normal for someone of her age but at least it had changed the subject completely and that was of paramount importance.

He hadn't even reached her when one of the ropes snapped and she was just at the highest arc of the movement, level with the old bough of the tree. There wasn't even time for fright. She fell like a leaf but there was nothing delicate about the way she hit the ground, and grass, however lush with summer growing, was not nearly soft enough to cushion the fall.

For a second she had no time to feel anything but pain and Ryan was kneeling beside her before she could move.

'Did you bang your head?' he asked urgently.

'No.' It was a bit of a gasp and his urgent concern turned to irritation.

'Let's be grateful for that. A blow is more than a head like yours could stand.' His hands slid over her carefully. 'Well, you seem to be in one piece.'

'I'm winded,' Lauren groaned, struggling to get up.

'You're also quite mad,' he growled. 'I fondly imagined you were grown up. I even offered you a whisky last night. I can see a reassessment is required.'

'You're being very sarcastic,' Lauren complained, still struggling, and he swept her into his arms, standing and making for the house.

'I'm being very annoyed,' he corrected shortly. 'Don't push me right now. I can promise nothing but violence.'

'I suppose it was stupid,' she conceded, trying to get comfortable against him, and all she got was another angry grunt.

'You're being very generous to yourself. Will you stop wriggling?' He glared down at her, his eyes a hard, clear green, none of the turbulent turquoise left that had been there before. He was annoyed for sure; that was what happened to Ryan's eyes when he was annoyed. She had good reason to remember.

'Please stop looking at me like that,' she asked a little anxiously. 'Your eyes go funny when you're angry and don't forget that I'm badly shaken.'

'You should be!' he snapped. 'One minute I was talking to a beautiful young woman and the next I was watching a mad child on a swing. How Redmond keeps up with your antics I don't know.'

'I don't have antics with Kent,' Lauren muttered, grimacing with pain, and the dark brows rose with very hostile enquiry.

'You were saving that up for me? Have you anything else planned?'

'It was spur of the moment,' Lauren assured him hastily as he walked into her bedroom and placed her on the bed. She looked at him a little warily as he pulled off her shoes and then stood staring down at her. It was a good job that nobody else seemed to be about because Ryan would not have behaved differently. He never pandered to people's sensibilities.

'Any injuries?' he asked coolly.

'A little twisted pride.' It brought a smile to his rather annoyed face and Lauren was pleased to see his eyes darken. They really were the most unusual eyes. Now the hard clear green was gone, and other, deeper shades were taking its place. Ryan's eyes were like the sea, turbulent, changing. Sometimes you never even noticed his handsome face because those eyes held you. They were holding her now with ease and he looked down at her sardonically.

'I'll get you a cup of tea. Lie still for a minute and get your breath back—and your pride.'

'If you hadn't insisted on joining me for a walk,' Lauren pointed out unfairly, 'I would never have considered jumping on the swing and acting as I did.'

'I drove you to it?' He shot her a sceptical look, his eyes moving over her face and the pale hair that spilled out around her on the bed. 'Was it something I said?'

He walked out and Lauren moved stiffly. She was getting her wind back but the pride would take a little longer and she wondered how on earth she could have behaved so idiotically. It wasn't anything he had said either. It was a treacherous memory that had suddenly surfaced at the mention of her first dinner-dance. It was astonishing that in all the six years she had never once thought of it before.

Olga walked in with a tray of tea and a worried expression on her face.

'Ryan says you had a fall. Shall I get the doctor?'

'A psychiatrist,' Lauren corrected. 'I went on the old swing and it broke. Ryan's none too pleased.'

'You've got to look at it from his point of view,' Olga reminded her. 'It must have been more of a shock to Ryan than it was to you.'

'I was the one who hit the ground!' Lauren looked at her in astonishment but Olga shrugged and made for the door.

'It must have been quite frightening to see you fall.'

Lauren swung her legs from the bed and sat up, still stunned by this way of looking at things. Come to think of it, everyone looked at things from Ryan's angle. Olga had a very casual attitude about the fall. It would have been nice to be fussed over. Olga was probably fussing over Ryan!

Lauren went for a warm shower and she couldn't find any bruises as a consolation. She was just coming back into her bedroom, wrapped in a silky robe, when Ryan walked in.

'Did you knock?' She was instantly on the defensive and her dark eyes regarded him with annoyance.

'I did. I see you've recovered enough to be starchy.' He walked further in and Lauren turned away, tightening her robe and reaching for her hairbrush.

'I'm still shocked and although it was my own idiotic fault I feel a little shaken, as I told you.'

'I expected as much. That's why I came back.' He walked up behind her, watching her through the mirror. 'I only left to order your tea and give you time to recover from your embarrassment.'

'I wasn't particularly embarrassed!' She turned to face him defiantly and he caught her slender shoulders in strong hands.

'You looked extremely flustered.' A long smile tilted his lips. 'What's the matter? Not getting enough attention?'

'I'm not a spoiled child!' Lauren scowled at him but as it only seemed to amuse him further she snapped out, 'In any case, I get plenty of attention from Kent.'

'But not here, not in your room in your own home.' He looked mockingly shocked, the goading look back with a vengeance, and Lauren tried to pull away.

'I'll get dressed and go down to find some attention. And, speaking of my room, you've no right to be here either.' The fact that he was there was making her feel decidedly uneasy. There was something about him that made her heart flutter alarmingly.

'But I've been here before,' he said softly. 'Remember?' He smiled with a certain amount of malicious satisfaction when her flushed face showed his barb had hit the mark and he walked out, leaving her with even more embarrassment.

He hadn't needed to remind her. It was the sudden memory that had sent her racing to the swing. Lauren sat at the dressing-table and brushed her hair, trying to get back into her character and out of the childish turmoil that Ryan had thrust her into. Being twenty-four was very different from being eighteen. She had had no poise then and she had been very immature at the side of Ryan. In any case, a first dinner-dance was an emotional occasion and if Ryan had been any sort of a gentleman he would never have mentioned it again.

While she was getting dressed she was quietly berating herself. It was something he would never have remembered if she hadn't put herself into this position. He would not have had to carry her to her room. He would never have been in her room. All her actions had done was underline the past, making him suddenly remember the night she had actually kissed him.

She looked at herself in the mirror and saw a cool, fair beauty, not a flushed, idiotic girl, but she kept her head turned away from the bed because that was where it had happened when Ryan had come to ask her if she had enjoyed herself. She had been sitting on the bed, bemoaning the fact that several ladies had demanded his attention when it was *her* night.

'What's wrong, baby?' Ryan had sat beside her but she had turned her face away. She was cross with him, disappointed, and she blamed him for the misery she now felt. She had never realised until tonight that she shared Ryan with other people. It had been made perfectly clear this evening, though. He turned her face back, looking rueful when he saw tears in her eyes.

'Crying? I thought you liked this evening. You looked beautiful.'

'Not beautiful enough,' Lauren said miserably. 'Nobody paid any attention to me.'

'That's not how it looked to me,' he said softly. 'Did somebody miss you out?'

'You did!' She looked at him accusingly and saw that wry twisted smile.

'I noticed,' he said quietly. 'A newly emerged butterfly, glittering and silken.' His voice was so soft and dark that Lauren's heart missed a beat and when he smiled warmly into her eyes she threw her arms round his neck, taking him by surprise, kissing him.

She still felt the embarrassment of the aftermath. For a moment Ryan had gathered her close, kissing her back, his hand cradling her head, quite scaring her. Not for long, though. He had looked at her seriously, still holding her.

'Don't make a habit of that,' he warned. 'Somebody might not realise that the beautiful creature is still a child.'

'I'm eighteen! You kissed me too!' She looked at him with great dark eyes and his own eyes narrowed in amusement.

'I thought I was supposed to. Isn't that what the tears were about?'

'I—I was overwrought.' She wanted to hide now because she seemed to have provoked Ryan into changing and she didn't want that at all. 'I don't want you to be different,' she added urgently.

Ryan laughed then, his green eyes darkening.

'When you grow up you'll be a dangerous female, Laurie,' he assured her softly.

She had taken about a year to get over that and had been very glad when Ryan went off to the States. He hadn't changed much after all. She grimaced; neither had she. There was still the tendency to act like a fool—

but only when Ryan was there. In London she was calm and sophisticated.

It was a pity that Ryan had come here on this weekend. It was spoiling things for Kent. She went down to find him. She would not wear jeans again while she was here. She smoothed down the skirt of her dress and looked at her slender image. This was how Kent knew her. It was a good job he had not been up this morning. Tomorrow morning she would linger in bed herself and Ryan could walk alone in the woods.

They were all having breakfast when she came in. Ryan and Kent got to their feet and Kent held her chair for her.

'Did you sleep in, darling?' he asked in amusement and Lauren smiled up at him sweetly.

'No. As a matter of fact, I've been up for some time.' She looked round the table, almost daring anyone to mention the swing episode, but it was clear that her mother didn't know about it and Olga was sitting with a very blank expression on her face that Lauren knew well. It was her 'It's not my place to interfere' expression, although she interfered readily if the mood was on her. She was probably still feeling sorry for Ryan. Lauren shot him an exasperated look but all he did was pass her the toast. She reminded herself that he could be very annoying. What did it matter? She was grown up now anyway. She had managed very well without him.

She spent the rest of the day with Kent. Normally she would have stayed around the house to have some time with her mother. Normally, too, she would have wanted to see more of Ryan before they went their separate ways again, but he was different. She wasn't sure at all that she would get on with him.

Kent wanted to see something of the countryside and they agreed to go out for lunch. To her annoyance he invited everyone else too but they declined, and when

Lauren went to her room to pick up a jacket she was still musing about the change in Ryan.

She still had many of her old things here at the house and impulsively she searched for photographs. There were many of her and almost as many of Ryan. Jack had been a very keen photographer. She found one without much searching and a smile came to her face as she looked at it. Nostalgia. Some memories were very good. There was Ryan, looking into the camera, his tilted smile just as she remembered him.

She frowned and looked more closely. He hadn't really changed at all except that he was older, harder. The eyes were the same, the dark hair. He had his arm draped round her shoulders and she remembered the photograph being taken. She was about sixteen then.

Lauren put it away. Maybe she was the one who had changed, grown up, grown distant. She shrugged in annoyance. There had always been this tendency to blame herself and not Ryan. He had been too much her hero, her friend. Well, she didn't need him and this homecoming had been a good thing. It had wiped away the childish fantasies. She had grown up away from him.

'He's not exactly what I expected,' Kent mused as they had a quiet lunch in a country inn.

'Ryan? What did you expect? I never mentioned him before.'

'The way you talked about him I imagined he would be softer.'

'There never was anything soft about Ryan,' she assured him. 'Where did you get that idea from?'

'The dreamy way you spoke about him,' Kent murmured. 'The way you greeted him. I was a bit miffed— slightly jealous.'

'About Ryan?' she looked at him in astonishment. 'He's family.'

'Not exactly,' Kent pointed out. 'He sounded more like your hero, a dream at the back of your mind.'

'I thought bankers had logical, prosaic minds?' Lauren scoffed. 'I hadn't imagined their thoughts ran to heroes. In any case, I grew up.'

'Since last night?' Kent enquired wryly. 'Have you been arguing with him?'

'Certainly not. We don't fight in this family. Curb your morbid curiosity and let's go.'

He grinned at her. This was more like Lauren, sharp and glossy. On second thoughts, he preferred it to the softened, gentle creature he had seen once or twice since they came down here. It would be a good thing when they left.

CHAPTER THREE

THE White House was a quite huge hotel a few miles away from Langbourne Manor. As a child, Lauren had been overwhelmed by it and even now it was impressive. Even pressure from Ryan had not succeeded in getting Olga to join them, which meant that they could all get into Ryan's car. Lauren would have preferred to go with Kent but she found herself sitting with him in the back while her mother sat with Ryan.

He still drove in the same way, she noted. Fast, skilful, never giving her a momentary qualm. He was too damned good at everything and she couldn't understand why she now found that irritating when before she had been proud of it. Their table had been booked early, which was a good thing as the place was crowded on Saturday evenings. An orchestra came down from London at the weekends because it was always full, and tonight was no exception.

'It's still quite exciting, isn't it?' Sylvia whispered, leaning towards Lauren as they took their seats at the table. 'I remember the flutter you got into the first time Ryan brought you here.'

So did Lauren. She had been remembering it all day. She shot a quick look at Ryan but he was busy talking to someone he knew. Nobody ever forgot him and Sylvia nudged Lauren as she too looked round.

'That's Veronica Marsh over there. Remember her? She was very struck on Ryan at one time. She must be all of thirty-two by now, married and divorced. She noticed him at once. I wonder if she'll try her luck again?'

'Mummy! You really are a wicked gossip,' Lauren muttered. She had noticed Veronica Marsh because it was like a recurring nightmare. It had been that woman who had precipitated her actions with Ryan so long ago. She certainly wished she had refused this honour when Ryan had mentioned it this morning.

'What are you two whispering about?' Ryan asked lazily, glancing at them, and before Lauren could take any action her mother behaved very true to form.

'We were looking at Veronica Marsh, dear. She married, you know, but she's divorced now.'

'I noticed her—very glossy,' Ryan said drily. 'Maybe I should have married her myself.'

'Well, you had plenty of chance but I'm glad you didn't,' Sylvia said comfortably. 'I found her much too hard. I don't think you liked her either, did you, darling?' she added, looking at Lauren.

'I never knew her,' Lauren said nonchalantly. 'She was much older and not in my circle.' She hoped her offhand voice would silence the chatter about the woman. It was ridiculous to be so embarrassed about something from so long ago. It would have been much better to come right out with it and laugh, but one look at Ryan convinced her she hadn't quite that amount of sophistication. He was smiling that odd smile, maliciously amused. She turned her attention to Kent and when he asked her to dance she almost leapt to her feet.

Trouble came at the end of the evening when she could no longer get out of dancing with Ryan. True to her mother's surmising, Veronica had pounced on him and he had seemed to be enjoying dancing with her. It was probably only her mother's remarks about not liking the woman that had prevented him from inviting her to join

them. She seemed almost to have abandoned her own
party at the sight of Ryan.

Now Lauren found herself on the floor, dancing very
unwillingly with Ryan, and he still had that mockery
about him. Her mind was so much into a defence mode
that his attack from an unexpected quarter quite startled
her.

'Is Redmond going to be able to keep you in the
manner to which you've become accustomed?' he enquired when she had just danced silently.

Her head shot up and she met sardonic green eyes that
probed into her mind.

'You're not any sort of guardian. I don't really think
it's your affair.'

'You *are* my affair, as I reminded you,' he said quietly.
'Along with your mother, I'm part owner.' The statement
stunned her and she stopped dancing but Ryan tightened
his hold on her and she had to move, but she couldn't
answer. 'So how is he going to keep you?' he went on
remorselessly.

'I never asked him,' Lauren managed tightly. 'We
don't talk about money.'

'Just about love,' he surmised scathingly. 'You're
wearing about two thousand dollars' worth of gown at
the moment, my pet. Can he keep that up, do you think?'

'I don't expect to be kept!' Lauren snapped. 'I'm not
a Victorian spinster looking for a suitable match.'

'Now who could compare a Victorian spinster with an
exotic, golden creature like you?' Ryan asked ironically.
His eyes flared over her, green and scathing. 'You're too
beautiful to be real. I somehow can't see you slaving
over a hot stove.'

'I told you that Kent has wonderful prospects!'

'And in the meantime? I'm considering the bread-and-
butter economics.'

'I work,' Lauren said hotly. 'I also have my allowance. I shouldn't think we'll have to fall back to bread and butter.'

'Just so that we understand each other,' Ryan murmured, dismissing the subject.

'But we don't, do we?' Lauren persisted. 'We don't understand each other any more.' She felt quite miserable now and not a little oppressed.

'Oh, I always understood you, Lauren,' he assured her quietly. 'The lack of understanding was yours.'

'Obviously. I'd never tell you my secrets now.'

'I already know your secrets.' He tilted her downcast face. 'I also know that you're too spoiled to take advice. Therefore I will not offer any. We'll just dance.'

'I no longer want to,' Lauren said stiffly, holding herself like a rod.

'I do.' He gathered her closer and danced with his face against her hair. 'The least you can do is keep me safe from Veronica, for old times' sake.'

It intrigued Lauren out of her mood and she looked up at him.

'Is she after you?'

He was smiling down at her, the hard green softened. 'I rather suspect she is. Luckily I'll be able to escape. I only have a week here. The last time she was after me, I seem to remember that you rescued me.'

'If you're talking about the jealous antics of a teenager on her first dinner-dance just say so out loud,' Lauren challenged, taking the bull by the horns. 'I remember too. I was frustrated at having my nose pushed out when it was my big night.'

'You certainly turned it into a big night,' he said softly.

'I was light-headed with the wine and greatly annoyed.'

Ryan just laughed and pulled her back to him and she was quite pleased with her little attack. It was better to have things right out. It was the lingering guilt that had made her be so stroppy with Ryan. Perhaps this rift between them was all her fault?

'Ryan?' She said his name softly and he bent his dark head closer.

'What is it, sugar?'

'I really don't want to quarrel.'

He never answered but a certain warmth came into his attitude and when the dance ended and they both saw Veronica making a bee-line for them Lauren stayed right where she was, dancing away with Ryan as the music started again.

'A friend in need ...' Ryan murmured and suddenly they were laughing, back to how they had been. Yes. It really was her fault after all, Lauren mused. Guilt. Ryan hadn't changed, it was her. It made her happy and she gave him an impulsive hug that gained his immediate attention.

'At twenty-four you may not get off as lightly as you did at eighteen,' he warned softly.

'It was a friendly gesture,' Lauren countered, smiling pertly into suddenly brilliant eyes. 'At twenty-four I can also take care of myself and I'm almost an engaged lady.'

She was very pleased with the whole evening. A lot of things had been dealt with, mostly to her satisfaction, and when she went to bed later she had the feeling of having set things right. She had set Ryan right too and that took some doing.

She went to her mother's room for a last gossip. She would be going tomorrow afternoon and she had not really had a good chat with her mother at all. The chat lasted an hour and she was just crossing the landing upstairs when she heard voices in the hall. Leaning over the banister, she was really surprised to see Kent there, still dressed, and the other person was Ryan.

'Olga said you wanted a word with me,' Kent was saying and Ryan agreed quietly.

'I do. Come into the sitting-room. Standing about in the hall is never a good idea in this house. Sound carries all over.'

The door closed behind them and Lauren was astonished. Kent and Ryan had been quite cool with each other. What on earth could they have to talk about? It didn't take much thinking out. Her! Ryan was not letting matters rest in spite of all she had said. She ran down the stairs in her bare feet and hadn't the slightest hesitation about eavesdropping. She was not a child to be discussed so arbitrarily.

As it was, she missed the beginning because Ryan, true to fashion, had got right down to it with his first words, and she had been quite right—he was still going on about Kent's prospects.

'Of course I can keep her comfortably.' Kent sounded quite stroppy and she nodded in satisfaction—good for him! 'I'm on my way up.'

'I would have thought that Lauren needed someone who had already arrived,' Ryan said coldly. 'She's used to a good deal of luxury.'

'Lauren works,' Kent snapped angrily. 'She's not exactly wrapped in cotton wool.'

'Lauren simply plays at working,' Ryan corrected icily. 'She always knows that at any time she can simply walk out and it makes a great deal of difference. Working for her living and helping you to climb higher would be a very different prospect.'

'It doesn't matter whether she works or not,' Kent said heatedly. 'I can keep us. In any case, you're not her father or her guardian. As far as I can see it has nothing to do with you.'

'I've spent a good deal of my life protecting her,' Ryan bit out. 'I'm not about to stop now.'

'She's completely independent. Working or not, she has a huge allowance.'

'I'm aware of it,' Ryan said quietly. 'Suppose she was to inform you that it would stop when she got married? How would you take to that?'

'I wouldn't give a damn! I love her and I'm going to marry her whether you like it or not.'

'Oh, I don't like it,' Ryan informed him with soft menace. 'I know Lauren. I don't think you are at all what she needs.'

'Too damned bad!' Kent stormed. 'Tomorrow we go back to London. I know her enough to be sure she'll do exactly as she likes. If you wanted to keep her under your thumb you should have taken her with you to America!'

Lauren could tell that as far as Kent was concerned it was the end of the interview and she flew upstairs on legs that were suddenly shaky. It wasn't fear, though. It was sheer fury. She couldn't believe Ryan's arrogance. Tomorrow she would have it out with him. If she tried to do that tonight she would feel like killing him! She had no tendency to take the blame for this.

Not wanting to have anyone else upset, Lauren realised she would have to waylay Ryan, and the time to do that was on the morning walk. She had not planned to take one but she was up early as usual, ready in her jeans and sweater and watching from her window for Ryan to come out of the house. When she saw him she raced down the stairs and let herself out quietly. This time she would be the one to suddenly appear!

He had already reached the trees and as she had made no move to be stealthy he saw her coming and waited.

'Somehow, I didn't expect to see you this morning,' he murmured as she came up to him. His eyes moved over her tight expression and narrowed at what they saw. 'I assume another fight is about to begin,' he added drily.

'Not yet!' Lauren marched off into the woods and he made no attempt to keep pace with her angry steps. Out of sight of the house she turned to confront him, her eyes blazing, and he came towards her slowly, watching her like a hunter facing a small but savage prey.

'Be advised,' he warned softly, 'I no longer consider you to be a child, and therefore childish tantrums may bring about grown-up punishment.'

'But you *do* consider me to be a child!' Lauren snapped. 'You believe it so much that you imagine you can interfere with my life!'

'Redmond is already up?' Ryan asked with sardonic astonishment. 'I really am surprised, or did he spend the night in your room, grumbling and complaining?'

Lauren lashed out at him furiously but her wrist was caught in a grip like steel and Ryan's eyes became a frozen green as he looked down at her.

'I've warned you,' he reminded her coldly. 'Don't bank on the past.'

'I think you're living in the past!' Lauren seethed, snatching her hand free. 'Kent is not up and he did not spend the night with me. I heard everything you said last night, and yes, I was eavesdropping. I had every right to.'

'Then you must have been pleased with his replies.'

'What else did you expect? It's not the replies that concern me, it's the questions. You have no right to question either of us. How we manage is our affair. I'm astonished that you imagine you can step out of the past and take control of my life.'

'You want to be a suburban housewife, counting the pennies and checking your groceries anxiously? Somehow I can't see it.'

'Second sight,' Lauren snapped, 'because I won't be doing it. As Kent pointed out, I work and I'm going to go on working. I also have an allowance that is as constant as a river.'

'And if it dries up?'

'It won't. It may interest you to know that I've often thought of refusing it but I can't see any purpose in that action as it would just grow alarmingly all by itself. Kent suggested that I refuse it.'

'That's interesting,' Ryan murmured scathingly. 'You're telling me that he advised you to cut yourself off without a penny?'

'*He* doesn't interfere with my affairs!' Lauren pointed out heatedly. 'He merely asked if I had ever considered it. I heard you tell him that if I married it may stop. You know nothing about it. It was arranged long before you knew either my mother or me.'

'Really? Now I didn't know that,' Ryan said softly. 'I thought it started when you were eighteen?'

'Of course it did! You imagine my father would have given me that allowance as a child to spend on chocolate? It was just amassing until then.'

'It surely did that,' Ryan drawled quietly. 'I believe you've built yourself quite a lifestyle in London.'

'Look!' Lauren said furiously. 'I object to your interference, I object to this conversation, I object to you! I only came out to tell you to mind your own business. I'll do exactly as I please and you'd better remember that.'

'I'll remember,' Ryan agreed quietly. 'Now I intend to walk and for once in my life I don't think I want you with me.'

Strangely, that statement really shook her. She didn't want to go with him, she was much too angry, but it was different when Ryan told her she was not welcome. He turned and walked off through the woods and Lauren watched him bleakly, her ready temper dying. She had been right to challenge him, of course she had. She hadn't said one single thing that was untrue.

All the same she had to fight hard not to feel a sense of desolation and she turned back to the house with unhappiness growing as her rage faded. She wished she had never come home at all. If Ryan had not arrived it would have been different but she had been so happy to know he was coming.

Now, for the first time ever, they had really quarrelled and she was left feeling bereft. The past had really died now and it would colour all her memories each time she came back here. It would be better to leave this morning. She didn't want the trauma of seeing Ryan all day.

He did not come in for breakfast and at first she was very glad but somehow it was a gloomy meal and she had visions of Ryan being almost as upset as she was over the affair. She pulled herself up sharply. Here she was again, excusing Ryan and blaming herself. She had always done it; that was what came of hero-worship. He was probably talking to somebody he had met, somebody else who doted on him, like Veronica Marsh. She wouldn't put it past that female to be hanging around for a glimpse of him.

After breakfast she sought out her mother and told her she was going back to London straight away.

'But Lauren, I thought you were staying until this evening?' Sylvia Landis looked at her mournfully and Lauren hugged her close.

'I know, but it would be better to go now, I think.'

'I did realise that Kent didn't look too happy this morning,' her mother pointed out. 'I don't think he likes it here much.'

It wasn't that, as Lauren very well knew. Kent was still smarting from his brush with Ryan. Oddly enough he had never said a word to her about it. Far from complaining as Ryan had surmised, he had simply kept it to himself. She couldn't bring it up either without admitting to eavesdropping and it was one thing to admit that to Ryan but quite another to tell Kent. He could be a little stuffy about things like that.

'Oh, Kent likes it here,' she lied, quite sure he did not, even before his argument with Ryan. 'It's just that I—er——'

'You've been quarrelling with Ryan,' Sylvia said. 'Don't look all mystified, darling. I know the signs. You never could face quarrelling with him. It just makes you miserable. Make it up, do.'

'I've no intention of making it up,' Lauren said firmly. 'It's not something I can forgive. Ryan had better realise he can't order my affairs now. I'm getting married before too long. I'm not a child. He's even interfering about the allowance Daddy left me.'

'You're probably wrong, dear,' Sylvia said. 'There—er—there's nothing to interfere with.'

'He's hinting that it might stop when I marry,' Lauren told her. 'Have you got anything written down about it that Ryan might have seen? The bank is infuriatingly vague about it. Doesn't your lawyer deal with it? It must be written down somewhere. I've never bothered much. I was just overwhelmed by it when I was eighteen and it simply goes on. It must have been some great investment to keep that allowance going at its present amount.'

'I—I don't really know. I suppose I could find out if you're worried.' Her mother had dropped into a vague attitude that startled Lauren. Far from being fluffy-headed as Kent had surmised, her mother was sharp as a needle, and Lauren looked at her in surprise. She didn't press it, though. Just mention any trouble with Ryan and her mother fell into gloom. Everybody did. She was probably thinking about that and not the allowance at all.

Kent was only too pleased to leave and Lauren was packing her case when Ryan walked into her room, and this time he definitely had not knocked. Lauren looked at him and then turned away.

'Did you want something?' she asked quietly, determined not to get into another quarrel. 'I imagine it's urgent as you just walked in without knocking.'

'I didn't take a chance on knocking,' he assured her grimly. 'I wouldn't be best pleased to have the door slammed in my face.'

'I'm perfectly civilised,' Lauren assured him tartly.

'When it suits you. I understand that you're going now. I take it therefore that you're ducking out. The fact that Sylvia rarely sees you is not bothering you at all.'

'You know perfectly well why I'm going,' Lauren said hotly, turning on him.

'Yes. You're going back into your dream world where nothing happens to disturb your glossy appearance. You're going back to drift along as usual. You'll probably drift into this marriage and then drift out of it again.'

'You're talking about me as if I'm a—a parasite!' She looked at him with a certain amount of horror and his tight lips tightened further.

'The expression is yours, and the thought,' he informed her angrily. 'I think you have no idea what you want. I told you if you had any intelligence you'd be dangerous. You're dangerous as it is, dangerous to yourself. You're emotionally illiterate!'

She forgot it was Ryan. She just flew at him, lashing out with her hands, beating at him frustratedly as he caught her to him and tightened his grip almost to pain. His arm was like a steel band round her and he fastened his other hand in her hair and pulled her head up, looking down into her face.

He wasn't annoyed and that quite frightened her. Somehow she had made a wrong move.

'So you *are* alive?' he pointed out mockingly. 'I was beginning to wonder. You like to have things all your way, though, don't you? Have you ever had a brush with Redmond of these proportions? How do you think he'd take it?'

'I expect you imagine he'd beat me,' Lauren seethed, struggling furiously. He tightened his hold until she gasped and he smiled down sardonically into her flushed face.

'I don't think he's capable. I imagine you'd win in a fight. Your temper would give you an advantage and he's so very nice, you'd be sure to catch him back-footed.'

She never had managed to take Ryan by surprise and she belatedly tried for dignity.

'You may let me go. I've recovered from rage. I now find your remarks merely contemptible.'

'Oh, Lauren!' He began to laugh quietly and his painful hold slackened. 'I wonder what you'll grow into?'

'I have grown!' Lauren assured him stiffly but it only amused him further.

'Have you, honey? I don't think so. I don't think we've made it there yet at all. That being the case, you should postpone this engagement until you really know your own mind.'

'Aha! Now we come to it.' She looked at him scathingly. 'I have to give you credit, Ryan. If one thing doesn't work you instantly try another. Unfortunately I know all your tricks.'

'Do you?' he asked softly. 'What about this one, then?'

When he bent his dark head and caught her lips with his, Lauren was too startled to resist. Her knowledge that he always did the unexpected had failed to encompass this at all and while her mind was still reeling he cradled her fair head and deepened the kiss, his mouth moving over hers with enough force to tell her he was not in any way teasing.

'Ryan!' She managed to draw back, recognising great danger, but he relentlessly pursued her and his name was still a gasp on her lips as his mouth captured hers again.

She was tensed up, almost panicking, too bemused to be annoyed, and it slowly dawned on her that he was not actually being aggressive. His lips were not insistent now, they were tracing her mouth with a feather-light touch, gentle, persuasive, and she felt a response growing inside that was easing away the tension. She had a tremendous desire to move closer, to let an urge deep inside her float free, and her hands moved to his arms, her fingers sinking into the soft wool of his sweater.

It was the low sound of triumph in his throat that alerted her to her foolishness and reminded her where she was. This was another ploy to get the better of her and she was falling for it like an idiot.

'You're despicable!' She wrenched herself free and looked up into darkened, amused eyes.

'But clever with it,' he goaded, watching her flushed face and the way her breast heaved with panic. There was a small pulse fluttering in her throat and his fingers reached out to it, finding it unerringly. 'I did warn you about grown-up punishment.'

'It wasn't punishment! It was——'

'A pleasure?' he interrupted drily. 'Well, at least it was something to remember me by. Do you still want me to give the bride away?'

'Just go, Ryan!' She turned away frantically and his short laugh was filled with contempt.

'Still playing? All right, Lauren, I'll go. I imagine it will be a long time before we meet again. In fact, it would perhaps be better if we never did. The past is long gone, isn't it?'

He walked out as quietly as he had come in and Lauren stared at herself in the mirror, at the hectic colour of her face, at her trembling hands. What had he expected to achieve by that? There must be something because Ryan never did anything for nothing.

She was ashamed at the way she had responded. She had grown out of that a long time ago. What if her mother had walked in? Ryan had not even bothered that the door was wide open. She saw it all then. He had wanted someone to see, but not her mother. He had wanted Kent to see. He disliked the idea of this marriage because he hadn't arranged it and that despicable little trick had been to put a firm wedge between Kent and herself.

He had deliberately worked her up and if she hadn't come to her senses she would have been locked in his arms right now with every possibility of Kent coming to find her.

Rage drowned out the last of the bemused feelings and she slammed the rest of her things into her case before storming down to find Ryan and tell him what she thought of him. If he imagined she would be too embarrassed he could think again!

'He's just gone out, dear,' her mother said as she stalked into the kitchen and demanded to know where he was. 'I'm not sure but I think he has a lunch date. It's probably that Veronica woman. Anyhow, he looked quite pleased with himself so I assume you've made up your differences?'

Lauren could imagine how pleased he was even though Kent had not walked into the trap. She said nothing, however, and when they were finally on their way back to London she felt as if she was escaping. Escaping! She had been dreamily enchanted to be back home; now she was actually fleeing. And it was all because of Ryan.

*   *   *

During the next few days she re-lived the weekend at home, going over each detail minutely in her mind because things were now completely changed. She felt as if she had cut herself off utterly from everything and everybody she had loved for so long.

She had actually done nothing of the sort and she knew it. She had only cut herself off from Ryan and looking at it logically she had been cut off from him for long enough; he had never even written to her after the first couple of years and after a while she too had stopped writing. It was really amazing that he thought he could step back and take up where he left off.

Gloom seemed to be surrounding her, though, and she knew it was more than that, deeper than that; even her mother had been odd at the end. She worried away at the problem and finally realised it had all stemmed from the time she had told her mother about her quarrel with Ryan and what they had quarrelled about. Her mother had been evasive after that and, come to think of it, she had never pressed them to stay. It was quite out of character.

It was not in Lauren's nature to let anything rest, though, and finally she had to know what was troubling her mother. She rang one afternoon, keeping things quite casual at the beginning. After an initial chat she brought up the subject of the allowance and this time, because she was attuned to it, she actually heard the change in her mother's voice.

'Well, no. I haven't found out anything, Lauren. It quite slipped my mind. I can't see that it's so important.'

'It is to me, Mummy,' Lauren said firmly. 'It's on my mind quite a lot and if you can't find out anything I'll have to come back and find out for myself. If this allowance is to stop when I marry, then naturally I want to know.'

Surprisingly, all she got was silence and knowing her mother she knew that some furious thinking was going on.

'Surely you were in on it when Daddy first arranged things?' Lauren persisted when her mother said nothing at all.

'Well, yes, I was. There was no mention of any marriage arrangement.'

'There you are, then!' Lauren said triumphantly. 'You could have told me that when I was there and saved me a lot of thinking. I expect you were too busy wondering if I'd upset Ryan.' She was not in any way being sharp; in fact she laughed. It was a relief to know that Ryan was wrong, and not for any other reason than that she suddenly felt a little more light-hearted.

Her mother did not laugh. There was this silence again and Lauren's laughter faded into worry.

'Mummy? What is it? Is something wrong?'

'I suppose there is really,' Sylvia Landis said quietly. 'It really doesn't matter any more what your father intended, Lauren. It hasn't mattered for quite a long time— since you were nineteen, actually.'

'What do you mean?' For no reason, Lauren's heart was beating like a drum and she asked herself why. She didn't care about the allowance—she could get a more regular job if the allowance stopped and Kent had said he didn't care; she had heard that herself. It was her mother's tone that was frightening her.

'Mummy!' She almost shouted. If something was wrong she wanted to know and Sylvia told her very reluctantly.

'Lauren, the allowance was supposed to see you to your twenty-fifth birthday. It was all carefully worked out and written into the will. Unfortunately it was in shares, the dividends to pay the allowance and a little of the capital to make it up each year.' She paused a second and Lauren could just imagine her biting her lip as she did when she was agitated.

'Look, it doesn't matter at all, but what happened?'

'The value of the shares just collapsed. It was while you were at college.'

'Just a minute. My life was pretty much arranged even to the finishing school. I didn't have a lot of choice.'

'It was what your father wanted, dear.'

'Perhaps so, but if the shares collapsed where did the money come from? Where is it coming from now?'

Even before her mother answered she knew. It was something she had never even thought of but suddenly it was all too clear.

'Ryan,' her mother said quietly. 'I made a solemn promise never to tell you. You were to go on as planned without any feeling of being beholden to him. He even increased the allowance. I think he threatened the bank with lawsuits and blue murder if they so much as let slip any whisper of it to you.'

This time it was Lauren who was silent. She couldn't answer and when she finally did her voice was husky with misery.

'So Ryan has been keeping me; he's keeping me now.'

'Does it matter, dear? He's always cared for you and, after all, he's probably a multi-millionaire. I've never queried Ryan. He's so clever. He always knows exactly what he's doing.'

Lauren could see that all too well. He had never let the reins go because he had been keeping her for years. She sat with the phone in her hand and looked round her beautiful flat. She loved it, felt a great deal of pleasure just to walk back into it each day. It was Ryan's. Everything was Ryan's. He probably owned most of her clothes.

'It does matter, Mummy,' she said quietly. 'This weekend, Ryan spoke to me as if I were a parasite. I can see now that I am.'

'Oh, Lauren! Do be sensible!' Her mother sounded exasperated. 'You really are being dramatic. Ryan is family.'

'No, he isn't, and it wouldn't make any difference, actually. I'm not blaming him in any case. I've never made any attempt to pull myself together. I've never quite got out of the finishing-school attitude. Of course now I'll have to. I need a full-time job. In fact, I need a career. I won't accept the allowance from now on.'

'And just what do you intend to do?' Sylvia asked sharply. 'You have to train for a career. What do you intend to live on until you're established?'

'I intend to do something I've been thinking of for some time,' Lauren said. 'I have quite a few qualifications and plenty of connections down here. I'll work as a high-class housekeeper, perhaps doing commissions where the need arises. I know somebody who does that and she's always in demand. Meanwhile, I'll get rid of the flat and take a room somewhere.'

'This is madness, Lauren!' Her mother sounded quite annoyed but there was no moving Lauren. She felt humiliated by several things. She had told Ryan to mind his own business. She had explained about her allowance as if he were a dim-wit and he had never corrected her. Small wonder he had said he was part owner of her. He had certainly paid enough.

There was no mystery about him questioning Kent either. He had no intention of keeping Kent. He probably wanted to choose her husband himself. Kent's reply must have infuriated him. That fact was her only consolation.

At least this had shaken her out of her restless attitude of just waiting. Ryan had forced her into that. If there had been no huge allowance she would have been like anyone else, working hard for her living. It was a thin excuse but she felt there was some justification in thinking it. Her dreamy adoration of Ryan had been childish memories and now they were gone. In her mind he was another person entirely, a cold, hard schemer.

CHAPTER FOUR

WHEN she had finally convinced her mother that nothing would move her from her plans, Lauren walked round the flat. It would be all gone soon and she might as well put it out of her mind. Most of the things in it had been paid for by Ryan's money. Very little was really hers, not unless she wanted to be a leech, a dependant, asking his permission for everything.

She rang her friend and talked about the new job she had planned. Apparently that particular business was booming. Many wealthy foreigners took houses in London and wanted someone fast; even cabinet ministers called on high-class housekeepers in an emergency. She knew she could do it and her friend gave her a number to ring that evening, somebody who was quite desperate for someone to begin next weekend.

It was happening so fast that Lauren felt a little scared but she rang and arranged an interview for the next afternoon. The die was cast. From now on she would be on her own. She never got the chance to tell Kent because he was away at a conference for a few days and wouldn't be back until the following evening.

So much the better. By the time she got in touch she would be another person and she knew he would approve. After all, he hadn't liked Ryan one little bit.

Lauren was up until the early hours because the whole thing had shocked her and she just couldn't sleep. Consequently she over-slept the next morning; in fact, she was still asleep when the doorbell rang violently. She had no time to come to her senses and she opened the door, her silky robe open over pyjamas, her fair hair tousled and her eyes sleepy, to find Ryan standing there looking as tall as a giant and furiously angry.

'Ryan! What do you want?' She was too startled and too bemused by sleep to be at all defensive and he glared down at her as she stood with the door slightly open, the safety chain keeping him out.

'I want words and I want them now! Don't try locking me out either or I'll create a scene that will take some living down.'

She quite believed he would and her initial desire to slam the door faded fast. She let him in and stared at him solemnly.

'You've been talking to Mummy——' she began but he interrupted harshly.

'Let's dispense with the obvious, shall we? As you've clearly just stepped from your bed, we'll also despatch Redmond to his bank before we talk.'

'Kent doesn't live here and if you're suggesting that——'

'I am perhaps presuming,' he conceded shortly. 'You're twenty-four, almost engaged and you live very well. Naturally I expect Redmond to share your good life.'

'Well, he doesn't!' She had to sharpen her voice although Ryan had her at a total disadvantage. To face him she would have needed a shower and her make-up on. She would also have liked some prior warning. He had descended on her like Nemesis. He looked quite alarming and she was still bewildered by sleep after a late night.

'Did you spend last night at a party?' he enquired scathingly, his cold green gaze raking over her.

'I did not!' In fact she was not much of a party-goer. 'I spent last night planning, all by myself, and now my plans are made and I know exactly what I'm going to do.'

'You're about to become somebody's housekeeper as I understand it, or has that plan changed?'

'It hasn't. I have an interview this afternoon.' She glanced at the pad by the telephone, just checking that she hadn't dreamed it, and the sight of the notes and the number reassured her. 'I'll pay you back all you've spent on me, however long it takes.'

'Are you trying to invoke violence?' he grated. His hands shot out and grasped her shoulders, his fingers biting into her through the thin silk of her robe and pyjamas.

'I'm trying to tell you that I'm quite capable of managing by myself,' Lauren said, looking up at him and trying not to tremble. He looked violently angry and she wished she didn't feel so defenceless. 'Today I'm having an interview for a job and I've every intention of getting it. Before I start and move into somebody's house for the duration of that job, I intend to get rid of this flat and all the things in it. The money can go towards paying you back. I'll take a room somewhere.'

'Why the desperation?' Ryan asked sardonically. 'You're getting married. Just move in with Redmond.' His scathing looks were beginning to get to her and she pulled free of his hands and moved away. 'Where are you going?'

His voice cracked out at her like a whip and she turned her head to look at him haughtily.

'I'm going to get dressed. Obviously I can't put you out without assistance. In any case, it's your flat.'

One long arm shot out and captured her again.

'You're not leaving my sight. It's not the first time I've seen you in your night attire. I'll not collapse. You can make me some coffee. I left without breakfast. When I've had the coffee you can feed me.'

'I'm not a servant!'

'You're planning to be one. Or am I not high-class enough? Tell you what, I'll pay you. Pretend you're my housekeeper until you've fed me.'

'You're impossible!' Lauren tried to get away but his hand tightened and he led her towards the open door of the kitchen.

'Too damned true,' he snapped. 'I intend to be even more impossible so you'd better make yourself some tea and blink the sleep from your eyes. All silky soft and astounded you're no sort of adversary. You stay right under my nose until some hard talking has been done.'

'You can't make me!' Lauren said hotly and he slanted her a very wry, green-eyed look.

'Don't make any bets on that,' he warned. 'I'm prepared to take any necessary action. I care a great deal for Sylvia. She's now worried and unhappy. Creating chaos is obviously your forte. Get a job doing that. Meanwhile, there's no way you're going into the houses of people you don't know, cooking them cherry pies and scrubbing their steps.'

'I shall do precisely as I please!' Lauren said calmly, making her hands work and getting the kettle on. 'This is all dramatic nonsense.'

'Time will tell,' Ryan warned. He sat on the edge of the table and watched her. 'Will you be getting breakfast for your masters looking like that or do you intend to wear a uniform?'

'You've got the whole thing wrong!' Lauren exclaimed angrily. 'I might have known you'd try to belittle me.'

'No,' he murmured threateningly, '*you've* got the whole thing wrong. Being a housekeeper is definitely out. There are several things you can be if you're intent on it but that is not one of them.'

'I'll decide!'

'After breakfast you'll decide,' Ryan informed her. 'Where are the cups?' He simply dismissed her anger scathingly and she felt frustratedly incapable of getting the better of him at the moment. It was because she was still half-asleep, she told herself. When she had got herself together she would be more assertive. Ryan could not now get to her. In her mind she had vanquished him.

Ryan sat drinking coffee, his eyes narrowly on her, and Lauren scrupulously ignored him. It was all she could do. She was well aware of her disadvantage and didn't mean him to know how shaken it made her feel. She prepared breakfast for him, quietly and methodically, and had nothing herself but the cup of tea she had poured. When she set the meal on the table she intended to just walk away but once again he ordered her to stay and she realised it was so that she would feel inferior.

That brought a defiant smile to her lips and she poured more tea and sat opposite as he ate. Two could play this game. If he thought pyjamas made her more subdued he could think again.

'That was wonderful.' He looked up at her as he finished the meal. 'That might just be the best breakfast I've ever had. I had no idea how good you were at this cooking business.'

'You haven't known me for a long time,' Lauren said quietly. 'Perhaps now you'll stop interfering and let me get on with my own affairs. As you can see, I can cope with meals. I can cope with just about anything else.'

'I wonder?' He looked at her intently. 'How will you cope when Redmond tells you the allowance was part of the marriage settlement?'

'He's not going to do that and, on second thoughts, I might just move in with him.' Lauren looked at him truculently, trying to stare him down, but the green eyes narrowed alarmingly and she sprang up before her nerve broke. Exchanging blows with Ryan in any way at all had never been a good idea.

'I'm going to shower,' she said stiffly. 'Let yourself out.'

'When I'm good and ready. Don't think you can run away from this. Even if I decide to go, I'll be back.'

'You'll have to be quick or I'll have moved out!' She snapped out the words and Ryan just looked at her evenly, his long fingers cradling his cup.

'Don't imagine for one minute that I'm going to let you make an even bigger mess of your life,' he growled. 'You've cut yourself off from common sense. I should have been back long ago.'

Lauren just stormed out of the room. He could make her feel inadequate and childish with a few well-chosen words. What she did with her life was nothing at all to do with him, and hadn't he assisted with her way of living by pouring all that money in her direction? If it was the last thing she did she would pay back every penny. The trouble was, there were a lot of pennies to pay back and Ryan was now a stranger.

When she came from the shower he was gone and she breathed a sigh of relief. At least she could think now without those green eyes following her every move. She had never realised quite how hard he was. The only good thing she could think of was that he would soon have to go. A giant business needed constant supervision and even Ryan couldn't be in two places at once.

It was almost time to go for the interview and she dressed carefully, sweeping her hair up and putting on a plain red suit. After looking at herself for a minute she changed. It looked too glamorous for the job. Finally she chose a navy blue and white check suit and by the time she was ready it was more or less the last minute.

She had to admit that she was nervous. For the first time in her life she had nothing to fall back on, no protection, and right now she needed it. She might not like this sort of job. She might hate the people. It was no use backing out now, though. Her pride would not let her and, even if it had, Ryan would be triumphant. She needed a job fast.

The house was tall and elegant, away from the constant rumble of traffic. It was in a quiet square where several foreign ambassadors lived and she wondered who this man was who wanted help so speedily. Mr Cartwright. The name rang no sort of bell.

It was a woman who opened the door and she didn't look too friendly.

'Yes?' She stared at Lauren and kept her firmly on the step.

'I have an appointment with Mr Cartwright. My name is Moore. I understand he needs a housekeeper.'

'Not any more.' The woman looked her over from head to foot. 'I can't understand why you're here, Miss Moore, in the circumstances.'

'I have an appointment!' Lauren looked at her in surprise. 'If you could let him know I'm here.'

'I am Mrs Cartwright,' the woman said coldly. 'Your agent cancelled your appointment, as you probably know. If you don't know then I can only suggest you keep a better control of things.'

'I haven't got an agent!' Lauren protested heatedly but her annoyance made not one bit of difference to the stiff-faced woman.

'Then all I can say is that your friends have a very distorted sense of humour. Be that as it may, we now have two other people to interview. Your appointment was cancelled and there the matter ends.'

'But there's some mistake,' Lauren said wildly. 'I can't understand this. At least let me attend the interviews,' she added desperately.

'I'm afraid not. Now that I've seen you, I can tell you you would not be at all suitable. We need someone who will really take over the house. You do not look capable, Miss Moore.'

'What's wrong with me?' Lauren snapped, temper overcoming her surprise. 'I have plenty of qualifications!'

'We do not need a fashion model, Miss Moore. We also need someone reliable and I can't say your behaviour has impressed me. I'll bid you good afternoon.'

Lauren never had the chance to argue further because the door was shut firmly in her face and for a minute she stood on the steps feeling quite dazed.

How on earth had this happened? She walked slowly away and it gradually dawned on her that she felt quite insignificant, humiliated. She had managed to get herself into a situation where somebody could stand there and give her a good dressing-down. From being a person who had no worries except for a feeling of being at a loose end, she was now in pretty deep water.

Nothing belonged to her, not even the money in the bank. She had to get a real job quickly and she had to move out of the flat. Not that Ryan would throw her out but she had stated her case very emphatically and there was no way she would go to him and beg.

She was still in a daze when she got back, her mind running around like a trapped bird, and when the phone rang she expected trouble. That was the state of mind she had got into. It was Kent and great relief flooded through her.

'I'm back, darling,' he said cheerfully. 'I've got a few things to do and then we'll have dinner. Can you meet me at my flat? We'll go on from there.'

'Oh, Kent! I'm so glad to hear your voice,' Lauren assured him. 'I've so much to tell you.'

'Later,' he laughed. 'I can't talk now. I've got to make a report. See you about seven.'

Lauren was smiling as she put the phone down but the smile died from her face as she glanced at the pad beside it. There it was, her appointment time, the telephone number and all the little details. The mystery was solved without any further searching. Ryan!

While she had been showering, Ryan had been acting. He had cancelled her appointment and he hadn't told her so that she could do something about it. Instead he had simply left and she had suffered that humiliation. How could he do this to her? Ryan had always cared for her. Now they were enemies and he would stop at nothing to get his own way. It stiffened her resolve as nothing else could have done.

She got ready in good time and took a taxi to Kent's flat. It was astonishing how she had changed in a few days. She was sure that Kent wouldn't even know her. Now she had big worries and her carefree attitude had quite gone. For the first time in her life she was anxious about money. Blithely saying she would refuse the allowance before she knew where it came from had been one thing. This was different because she had stepped off into thin air. She felt like an unwelcome tenant in her own flat. She even felt uneasy about the clothes she wore. It was like waking up to find that her past life had merely been a dream.

Ryan had been a dream too. She was really finding out just what sort of a person he was and the only word that described him was hard. He had been quite content to let her play but the moment she had made a move to get engaged and take her life on a path he had not chosen he had stamped down hard. If she hadn't found out about the source of the money he would no doubt have told her. Her only consolation was that Kent would shrug his shoulders and dismiss it as unimportant.

Kent was almost ready. He let her in and gathered her close, kissing her deeply.

'I've missed you,' he murmured against her hair. Lauren clung to him fiercely. She had missed him too. She could have done with him being there when she tackled Ryan. 'I'll get you a drink,' Kent said, letting her go. 'I just have to get my tie and jacket. We can talk over dinner.'

'Well, I've got plenty to talk about,' Lauren murmured, moving into the flat and smoothing her hair in front of the mirror. 'I've had several shocks.'

'What with, darling?' He wasn't really listening. She could see him through the mirror and he was paying little attention to her. If he had come back to her and been really interested her next move would perhaps have been different but as it was she dropped the bombshell with no warning.

'I'm broke. In fact, I've been broke for most of my life but I didn't know it.'

It gained his attention instantly and he turned to her with nothing else on his mind.

'What are you talking about?'

'I'm talking about my allowance. It's stopped as from now and I'm going to pay it all back.' Lauren turned to look at him and he just stared at her uncomprehendingly.

'You'd better explain.' He handed her a drink and poured one for himself and Lauren sat facing him, not at all sure now about how he would take this. He seemed to have gone very still. He hadn't dismissed it at all.

'I know now that the allowance came from Ryan,' she said quietly. 'Daddy's money ran out when I was nineteen and nobody told me. Ryan has been keeping me ever since. To be quite fair, the flat, my jewellery, my clothes and just about everything I own came from Ryan.'

'Why didn't your mother tell you?'

'Apparently, Ryan threatened everyone, even the bank. I was not to know.'

'And now he wants it back,' Kent said slowly.

'He doesn't. I'm paying it back, though. I feel humiliated enough as it is without knowing that Ryan practically owns me. I was all lined up for a job interview this afternoon. Ryan cancelled it as if he had every right. He never told me and I felt like a fool when I got there.'

'What sort of a job?'

'A housekeeper. Does it matter? The point is he cancelled my interview without consulting me at all. I intend to move out of the flat and take a room somewhere. I can just about manage that with my present earnings. I must get a good job, though, because I'll pay back every penny.'

Lauren was beginning to feel upset. Kent was taking this very seriously and she couldn't understand why. As far as she was concerned this had just been a good excuse to let off steam and have his shoulder to lean on. Far from being sympathetic he looked quite grim.

'So your allowance has stopped?' He got up and walked about with his drink. 'You can't make an adjustment from one sort of life to another overnight, Lauren.'

'I'll have to. What does it matter anyway? You suggested I give it up.'

'No, I didn't,' he corrected. 'I asked if you'd ever thought about giving it up. Why should you give up money? Why should anyone? Money is a damned good thing to have. Think what a difference it would have made to us, for example. I have to keep up a good lifestyle if I'm to rise in the bank. I'm not some little clerk. I've got a good future. With money it's possible to keep up with things, be seen in the right places, make an impression. With your allowance and both of us working we could have been flying high.'

'I'll be working,' Lauren pointed out, her heart sinking at his coldly calculating assessment.

'As a housekeeper? Really, darling! What do I say if anyone asks me what you do? Do you honestly think I could tell them you kept house for somebody?'

'I wouldn't be a common-or-garden housekeeper!' Lauren said heatedly.

'It's the same word, whatever you're doing. They would immediately think of you differently. When we went out to any dinners they'd be looking at you and smirking to themselves. I know how they are.'

'Is that because you're like that?' Lauren asked bleakly and he shrugged this time, angrily.

'Don't twist my words, Lauren. This has got to be thought out carefully.'

'Why has it?' Lauren asked sharply. 'It's my allowance that's lost, not yours. I heard you telling Ryan that it didn't matter.'

'You were listening?' Kent went red and looked quite shocked and it frustrated her even more. Ryan had just made some sardonic remark and let it drop. He hadn't been shocked.

'Why not? You were both talking about me. Would you have wanted to keep the allowance forever if it had been Daddy's money?'

'Of course I would!' Kent snapped. 'Nobody in their right mind gives money away. With money behind you, the sky's the limit.'

'I see.' Lauren looked down at her hands. This had not gone at all as she had expected. She had the cold feeling of being right out in the wilderness on her own. 'When we get married we can both live here and that will save money. I suppose I could get another kind of job. I could start a catering business.'

'Without capital? Do be sensible, Lauren.' Kent shot her an exasperated look. 'You can be infuriatingly

scatter-brained. I know you've got stacks of qualifications but you have absolutely no training and no experience.' He looked round impatiently. 'This is a
bachelor flat. With both of us in it we'd go mad. We'd
be under each other's feet all the time and I like room
to myself. We would need a house, money again! Quite
obviously we can't get married straight away now.'

Lauren looked at him with disbelief.

'So this money did mean a lot to you?' she said bitterly. 'In spite of the things you said, you were banking
on it.'

'You're twisting things again!'

'Am I?' She stood and faced him. 'What about our
engagement?'

'What's the point at the moment?' He turned impatiently away. 'We can just go on as before until things
sort themselves out a bit.'

'They're not going to sort themselves out,' Lauren said
flatly. 'I'm now penniless. I'll be penniless until I earn
money and I'll never be able to earn money to the extent
that Ryan has given me money. If you're expecting a
miracle, forget it. Ryan only makes miracles for himself.'
She walked to the door and opened it. 'I'll ring you in
a few days when you've had time to recover from the
shock.'

'Lauren! Will you stop being idiotic!'

'Do you know, Kent, I'm tired of people telling me
that I'm idiotic, childish, spoiled and every other damned
thing they throw at me?' She turned on him with furious
eyes. 'What I've been guilty of is playing with life. I'm
just finding out that it's not a game. If you find an
heiress, don't feel at all constrained!' She slammed the
door and went before the tears that had been threatening
could materialise and it was very significant that Kent
let her go.

She wanted to hide away now and lick her newly acquired wounds. She went straight back to her flat and Kent neither came nor rang. When she rang him, he was out, and she knew without second sight that he had gone out to dinner and left her to stew in her own troubles. It was just about the last straw. She made herself some tea and sat with it in her hands, the tears that had been threatening for hours standing in her eyes.

When the doorbell rang she thought it was Kent and she jumped up to answer it, brushing the tears away quickly. He had come to see if she was all right. It must have been a shock to him after all.

It was Ryan and she didn't have the chance to keep him out. He walked straight in and looked at her intently.

'Your eyes are red,' he said quietly. 'Your mascara is smudged too.' Lauren just turned away, feeling very raw and defenceless, and Ryan followed her into the sitting-room and stood watching her.

'So he wanted the money?' he surmised softly. 'Are you still moving in with him?'

'No. And if you've come here to goad...'

'I haven't. I've come here to see that you're all right and you know it.'

'I don't know it!' Lauren looked up at him with accusing, dark eyes. 'You've always...'

'Cared for you,' he finished firmly. 'I care for you now and you know that too, even though you won't admit it. Try to look at things logically for a change. Did you really expect me to give an allowance to Redmond? Did *I* inform you about the source of the money? Have I asked you to vacate this flat? The flat is yours. What the hell would I want with it?'

'It's worth a lot and...'

'It's peanuts! My only concern is that you don't make any further mistakes and Redmond is a mistake.'

'And what if I love him?' Lauren asked bitterly. 'What then?'

'Then I'm sorry for you but it makes little difference. He's just proved his worth, hasn't he?'

'It's all right for you to take a lofty attitude when you're rolling in money,' Lauren pointed out angrily. 'Kent says we would have to keep up a high standard. You'd feel the same if you weren't so rich.'

'Would I?' he grated. 'If I loved someone I'd be willing to sleep in a tent in a field just to be with her. My high standard would be seeing her smile. How I felt about her would colour all my days. Anyone who doesn't feel that doesn't know love. If you want a tidily arranged marriage with somebody calculating like Redmond then go ahead!'

'I don't,' Lauren whispered. His words had quite shaken her. She had never thought of Ryan being in love. The passion in his voice had reached right down inside her. It was no use being foolish about Kent either. She had changed so very rapidly. Now she was no longer playing at life and Kent looked like part of her past. When she had wakened from the dream he had begun to fade with it. Their relationship was something she had drifted into as she had drifted into most things.

'Then he can get himself another sleeping partner, I take it?' Ryan grated.

'I've never slept with him,' Lauren muttered vaguely, her mind still trying to sort out new feelings.

'And don't you find that odd?' Ryan asked quietly. 'If you found it easy to forgo then you've come to your senses in the nick of time.'

'Perhaps,' Lauren conceded. 'It doesn't change things, though.' She suddenly remembered his crime. 'You cancelled my appointment,' she challenged. 'I looked a fool when I went there.'

'I doubt that,' he mused, suddenly grinning down at her. 'You probably looked very aloof and superior. Don't take it to heart. You would never have got the job. No woman wants a beautiful lady around the house. If the man had hired you, she would have fired you.'

'That's not the point,' Lauren said hotly. 'You cancelled my appointment.'

'I did. You're not waiting on somebody hand and foot. I'd lock you up first.'

Lauren stared at him blankly and then looked away. She had to sort things out and now she wasn't even angry with Ryan. She wasn't anything except possibly very tired.

'I'm going to bed,' she muttered.

'After dinner.' Ryan swung her to face him and his expression softened as he looked down into her miserable eyes. 'Fix your face,' he said softly. 'We'll go for a quiet meal and we'll talk.'

'You just want to try ordering me about again,' Lauren said bleakly.

'You think so? Haven't I told you that I no longer consider you to be a child? I've been thinking about you all day. I can't seem to get that breakfast out of my mind. I want to offer you a job.'

'You need a cook?' Lauren asked derisively and he tilted her chin, smiling down at her.

'Something much more challenging than that,' he promised. 'Fix your face.'

Like it or not, she found herself going with him and she had to admit that with Ryan she tended to submit to fate. He had always had a hold on her and it seemed to have tightened now.

The restaurant was quiet, dimly lit, and she was grateful for that. She didn't feel up to the glare of bright lights. In fact, she was quite exhausted with the whole day. Ryan just let her relax, not saying very much, glancing at her from time to time, and she gradually felt better.

It was difficult to remain angry with him. In any case, she had taken all the blows at once and she didn't feel equal to a fight. She had the feeling that he knew it and she was well aware that Ryan was danger. Keeping quiet was a fairly good idea.

When they were having coffee, he brought up the subject of the future.

'Are you still determined to give up the flat and strike out on your own?'

'At twenty-four, I think it's time,' Lauren said quietly. 'In any case, you know I'll not let you keep me now I know.'

'Personally, I can't see why not,' he murmured. 'As you pointed out, I'm rolling in money. I give you very little actually.'

Lauren laughed a little bitterly.

'Oh, yes! Only enough for me to be called a poor little rich girl.'

'Who called you that? Redmond? Forget him. We're not here to talk about him at all.'

'What are we going to talk about, then?'

'You.' He looked at her intently, the light catching the glittering green of his eyes. 'If you're serious about a job, then I've got one for you.'

'I don't want favours, Ryan!'

'It's no favour. It's something I've been thinking of for a long time as a matter of fact. You've put it right at the top of the agenda. You're planning a job looking after people. I have enough people to keep you right on your toes.'

'I don't understand.' A little shiver ran down her spine. He looked serious and he looked vibrant. It was Ryan at his most dangerous and oddly enough it excited her.

'The Landis Group have many irons in the fire,' he reminded her. 'There are lots of companies that on the surface seem self-sufficient but in actual fact I own them, or rather the Group does.'

'You are the Group.'

At Lauren's wry remark he gave a lazy shrug. 'So I'm told. Be that as it may. As you can imagine there are constant meetings for all manner of things, meetings that are important where details are thrashed out and decisions made.' She nodded and he went on, 'People come from all over to the meetings, as well as the staff at the company in question. They eat!'

'What?' Lauren sat up straight and he grinned at her.

'They require lunch. However irritating, people have to be fed and it's a damned nuisance. Tables have to be booked, there's travelling to and from the restaurant and this tendency to linger over drinks. By the afternoon, most of them are sleepily replete and the work goes damn.'

'I'm to make them sandwiches?' Lauren looked startled and Ryan's lips twitched in amusement.

'No. You are to present them with fabulous food, right on the premises. No grumbling possible, no escape allowed, back to work on the gong. It will save money and time and relieve me of a lot of annoyance.'

'Just a minute.' Lauren stared at him in astonishment. 'You're serious?'

'Absolutely.'

'But—but it would mean going with you. It would mean going to—to California!'

'And several other places. If you're working for me then naturally you'll be where I am. That's where the action is.'

'You're wanting to keep an eye on me?' Lauren's face was flushed and her eyes were beginning to sparkle with resentment.

'Oh, I'll keep an eye on you until I know you're capable of doing the job,' Ryan assured her drily. 'I don't much like fiascos. After that, I'll be too busy and, more often than not, miles away.'

'I—I'm not going to do it,' Lauren stammered nervously. California seemed to be a long way off suddenly. She was quite used to travel but that had been when she could just go off by herself or with friends, secure in the knowledge that she had plenty of money and a firm base in England. This way she would be at Ryan's mercy.

'You mean you're not at all sure of your capabilities when the chips are down?' he asked scathingly and she glared at him.

'I mean I'll feel unsafe.'

'With me?' He looked at her askance and she flushed more than ever.

'You know perfectly well what I mean. I'll have no place to run to if you—if you start getting awkward. How do I know it's not just a way of keeping me out of mischief? How do I know you're not treating me like a half-wit who has to be under your thumb?'

'I don't want you under my thumb. Lauren,' he said quietly. 'We help each other. I need help in this and it's all very real. As to your being there, I want you there. I've missed out on a lot of your life.'

'It's my life!' Lauren told him firmly but all she got was a derisive smile.

'What's the matter? Haven't you the nerve to live it fully? Would you rather drift as you have been doing?'

'I'm not going to drift. I'm getting a job.'

'And what about the job I'm offering?'

'I—I'll think about it.' Deep inside she wanted to go. It sounded challenging. She didn't know if she could do it, though. It would take a great deal of organisation.

There was Ryan too. He scared her a bit. There was an intensity about him she had not seen before and she felt her present position all too keenly.

CHAPTER FIVE

LAUREN was silent on the way back to her flat and instead of just dropping her off Ryan came in with her.

'Surely you're going to offer me a coffee?' he asked wryly when she looked startled. There was nothing she could do but agree. After all, it was really his flat, even though it was peanuts.

Lauren went to put her coat in the bedroom and the doorbell rang before she could get back. She heard Ryan go to answer it and when she came hurrying out Kent was standing there, just inside the flat, and he was looking daggers at Ryan.

'So you've been out?' he challenged. Lauren was really surprised. What had he expected her to do, sit and scream?

'Yes, I have. I went out to dinner. I imagined you'd gone out too.'

'I did, but I thought you might be unhappy about things. I called round to talk it over.'

Suddenly she was annoyed, very annoyed. Kent was behaving as if he were doing her a favour.

'Did you bring me the scraps in a doggy bag?' she asked tartly. 'Obviously you thought I'd be here sunk into gloom and underfed.'

'Do you think we could talk without onlookers?' Kent asked angrily, glaring at Ryan, who leaned against the door with a look of great interest on his face.

'Oh, I'm not just looking, I'm listening,' Ryan pointed out sardonically.

'We'll talk tomorrow, then, Lauren,' Kent said stiffly, preparing to go. 'We'll decide what to do.'

'I told you what I'm doing,' she reminded him, 'I'm going to be a housekeeper.'

'You can't! I've explained why. In any case, you'd probably get as far in any interview as you did today,' Kent snapped. 'You have no experience and nobody is about to set you on as anything of the sort.'

'Well, I've offered her something of the sort,' Ryan murmured and Kent shot him a furious look before turning back to Lauren.

'Don't tell me you're going to keep house for him like an old maid,' he rasped insultingly. 'He just wants you where he can tell you what to do.'

'I've been offered a job catering for the whole Landis Group,' Lauren informed him, furious at this further scathing attack on her. She was looking at Kent with entirely different eyes and she knew she had only just woken up. It was like coming to life after a long sleep. From now on, nobody would get the chance to be scathing. She was taking matters into her own hands.

'I know you,' Kent scoffed. 'You'll never leave London and the bright lights. He's wasting his time trying to persuade you.'

'You're wrong,' Lauren said quietly and firmly. 'I hadn't made my mind up but now I have. I'm going with Ryan.' She was very sure. More sure than she had been in the whole of her life and it was like a weight lifting from her. She would take a chance, and who better to take a chance with than Ryan?

'He'd do anything to keep you under control,' Kent snapped. 'He's even pretending there's a job.'

'Oh, there's a job all right,' Ryan assured him softly, 'and I think she can do it. In any case, she'll try and I want her with me. She seems to have developed a keen sense of observation recently,' he added scathingly. 'She learned to recognise a social climber.'

Kent walked out and slammed the door and Ryan looked at her closely.

'Will you be able to sleep?' he asked quietly.

'You bet!' She was steaming with anger but she even recognised that she was different herself.

'Then forget the coffee. I'll go. Tomorrow we'll discuss the new job, unless you just said that to get the better of Redmond?'

'I'd like the job,' she assured him a little tremulously and he nodded as he turned to the door.

'You've got it. Interview over. I'll see you tomorrow.'

Lauren suddenly felt a great wave of panic, not at all sure if she could sleep after all. She had committed herself to a very big project in a new place. She would only know Ryan and they had grown apart.

'Please don't go, Ryan!' The plea just seemed to burst from her and he turned at the door to look at her quizzically.

'Another change of heart? Was the speech about going with me just to put him in his place after all?'

'No. I meant it. I want to go, really.' She turned away a little anxiously. Now that she had begged him to stay she didn't exactly know what to ask, what to talk about. Ryan leaned back against the door and looked at her steadily.

'So why the frantic desire to keep me here?'

'I'm sorry. You're probably tired.'

'I'm rarely tired,' he corrected. 'However, from time to time I get suspicious.'

'From time to time I get panic-stricken.' Lauren turned to face him and took a deep breath. 'I just didn't want you to go. I've got this feeling of stepping off at the deep end. I—I just wanted to talk about things. After all, I don't know anything about it. I mean, how soon will I have to start? What type of food? What about suppliers? What about——?'

'I'm leaving all that to you, honey,' Ryan interrupted seriously. 'Your mission will be to relieve me of a burden, not add to it.' He looked very adamant and Lauren's face fell, her lips parting in dismay.

'But I won't know...'

Suddenly he was laughing at her, levering his lean body away from the door and coming towards her.

'Make the coffee and I'll tell you,' he suggested softly and she knew she had just been subjected to one of Ryan's endless attacks of teasing.

'Why do you do things like that to me?' she asked hotly, glaring at him.

'What are friends for?' He cupped her face in his hands and looked down at her mockingly and Lauren found herself smiling in spite of everything.

'I'll get the better of you yet,' she threatened, looking up into the changing green eyes.

'One of these days,' he agreed softly. 'What about the coffee? I can't plan a thing without it.'

It was three in the morning before Ryan finally left and by that time they had talked over every aspect of her new job. It had been a serious discussion but it had done a great deal to bring them back to their old relationship. Lauren had made them a late supper and she had curled up on the floor by Ryan as they talked. She was now settled in her mind about going, excited and looking forward to the challenge.

'Don't start sorting out recipes now,' Ryan ordered as he went to the door at last. 'There's a fanatical gleam in your eyes but it's three in the morning.'

'I'd no idea it was so late!' Lauren looked stunned and Ryan's lips quirked.

'Time flies when you're having fun,' he said drily.

'Oh! I probably bored you,' Lauren exclaimed guiltily.

'You've never bored me in your life,' he assured her. 'I get endless amusement just watching you.'

She wasn't quite sure how to take that and she looked at him warily but all she got was that enigmatic smile that might mean anything.

She locked the door, put the chain on and went slowly to the bedroom. She might regret this later. She might regret it very bitterly but it was a challenge, the biggest of her life, and she knew she was safe with Ryan. It was something she had learned all over again. He might be a little scary now and he might be dangerous but he would not let her sink. It was as good a way as any of learning to cope with real life.

So far she had escaped irritated bosses. Ryan would be the most irritated boss in the whole world if she let him down. She wasn't even sure if he would be patient at the beginning. Well, she had boasted about her abilities. Here was where she put it to the test. If the worst came to the worst he would send her off home but at least she would have seen California. And this evening had made her sure of one thing. If she was in at the deep end, Ryan would be watching, and that made her feel safer than anything else could have done.

Ryan insisted that they discuss it with her mother. He was round next day and found Lauren standing disconsolately in the middle of her sitting-room.

'A problem?' He looked at her sternly and she could see he didn't trust her completely. He still thought she might back out of it. Of course, the old Lauren might well have done that but she was different now. It didn't mean she had no problems, though.

'If we're leaving for California in two days I have to get ready, to pack and—and things...'

'Something stopping you?' he asked, standing by the door and looking at her rather coolly.

'I've got a lot of things,' she pointed out uneasily, very much aware now that Ryan had provided them. 'I can't take everything. I'll have to arrange storage and that takes time.'

'It's a funny thing,' Ryan mused sardonically, 'I imagined this flat could be locked and left. You object to your surplus possessions being here?'

'It's not my flat,' Lauren muttered, blushing for no good reason. 'There's the matter of selling it.'

'Ah!' Ryan eyed her severely. 'Tenacious, aren't you? This is your flat. The belongings are yours. I can't see any reason why the two should not be left together to wait.'

'You know I can't keep it now that I know,' Lauren reminded him a little desperately. 'We've been through all that.'

He just stared at her for a minute, and it seemed to be a very long minute because his eyes had gone clear, hard and vivid green again. Lauren gulped nervously. She didn't want a row with Ryan, not after they had managed to get on well last night and particularly as she had agreed to go with him.

'Would honour be satisfied if I made it part of the job?' he finally enquired.

'How do you mean?' She could see he was struggling with extreme annoyance and she assumed that to Ryan this was somewhat petty. It was not petty to her, though. She wanted a new beginning.

'I mean that there are various perks to any job. Let's call this a perk to the job you'll be doing for me.'

'But it's expensive! I mean it's not like—like luncheon vouchers!'

'Well, no,' he agreed seriously. 'On the other hand, I aim to get more value out of you than I would from someone who just warranted luncheon vouchers—not that I hand them out,' he added wryly.

Lauren bit her lip and looked away. It would solve her problems, all of them. It was overly generous, though.

'I feel guilty about it,' she confessed, looking up. 'I'll still feel that you're keeping me.'

'I've told you, it's to be part of the job. As to keeping you,' he added softly, 'I can afford you. I'd gladly keep you for the rest of your life.'

'Why, Ryan?'

'Family ties, friendship and the reflected glory of helping to rear the family swan,' he said quietly. He looked round impatiently, evidently bored with the trend of the conversation. 'Let's call it settled. Now we go to see Sylvia and assure her that you will be safely chaperoned and seriously hard-worked. Get your bag.'

It was the end of the conversation and Lauren felt a little overwhelmed. If she ever had to fight Ryan on his home ground she would come off badly and she knew it.

'You're a bit worrying,' she murmured, going to the door obediently. 'I hope you're going to continue to be on my side.'

'I never remember the time when I was not,' he said imperiously, ushering her out and locking the door.

'Well, we had a good long fight over the weekend,' Lauren pointed out.

'Just settling back into our old routine. Things have now adjusted themselves.'

'To *your* satisfaction!' she reminded him a little tartly.

'Naturally! That's why I came back to England.'

'You came to stop me from getting engaged?' Lauren stood by his car and stared at him in disbelief.

'To stop you from making a mistake,' he corrected. 'And it would have been a mistake, wouldn't it?'

'That's neither here nor there...' she began stormily, but he took her arm in a hard grip and stared down at her.

'Wouldn't it?' he repeated insistently and Lauren's eyes fell before the green fire.

'Yes.'

'Then can you tell me why we're standing here arguing? This tendency you have to go for the jugular will have to be curbed. Into the car. I haven't all day.'

'You'll probably be impossible to work for,' Lauren grumbled, obeying the command.

'Then you'll leave, sugar, and I'll just keep you in luxury,' he taunted. He got in and pulled away and Lauren sought frantically for a stinging reply but nothing occurred to her. When she muttered to herself in annoyance he just laughed.

A week later, Lauren stood on the balcony of Ryan's house in California and looked out over the rocks. Whatever she had expected it had not been a house like this. It was white, spacious, like a great ship at sea, and it stood on a rocky headland that faced the rolling breakers of the Pacific Ocean.

'Why here?' she asked. The whole thing had been a surprise and she was not at all settled to it yet.

'Because it all began here,' Ryan said quietly, coming out to stand beside her and handing her a long cold drink. 'Not here in this specific place but fairly close by. This is where my grandfather built his small empire and finally this was the house he owned.'

'It's beautiful,' Lauren said softly. 'I'm astonished your father ever left this place.'

'It wasn't his. My uncle inherited the house—he was older. Of course, he never married, and that's how I came to get everything. Grandfather tied it all up neatly. If he hadn't I would now be battling with strangers for my inheritance, probably a cats' home, because although they were brothers there was no love lost between Dad and my uncle. That's why Dad just stayed in England after he married Sylvia. She's never seen this place.'

'Which is a great pity,' Lauren mused.

'We'll invite her out.' Ryan was standing looking out to sea and Lauren glanced at him uneasily. Things were not quite as she had expected. Ryan had never said anything about this fabulous place and she had assumed that he lived right in the middle of some city. As it was, they were several miles away.

The fact that she was living here too was a matter of grave concern. She had imagined that some sort of living accommodation would go with the job and Ryan had agreed that it would. When it had finally got down to details he had simply said, 'You'll be with me.' It had been a little too late to pull out then and here she was, right beside him. Upstairs she had a huge room that looked out over the ocean and she could not have wished for more luxury, but nevertheless she was on edge both about her job and about Ryan. If anything went wrong with the job she would have to live with it here too.

Of course, if she couldn't cope or if tempers got frayed she could demand to go home like a bad-tempered brat but it would be putting her right back where she had started and once again she would be refusing to face up to things. She knew she would not run, no matter what the problems.

Her mother had been delighted about everything and Ryan had scooped Lauren away like a magician. Well, it was gloriously warm, sunny and peaceful and tomorrow she was going to be introduced to her responsibilities. She might as well relax now and make the most of it. She sighed and Ryan glanced at her.

'You're just a little scared,' he surmised.

'Yes, but I'll manage. I can't think what I'm worried about really. Cooking is cooking and I love it. I'll cope with the numbers.'

'You'll have a horde of assistants,' Ryan informed her and she spun round to face him.

'You never said that!'

'I've said it now. Did you imagine you'd be catering for anything from ten to thirty people and washing up later? You're the glamorous chief, not the kitchen slave.'

'This is assuming worrying proportions,' Lauren told him, her eyes definitely anxious. He leaned back against the rail and smiled his long sardonic smile.

'It's a big job for a big girl. I don't want a servant, Lauren, I want help. When you've got your hand in I'll probably add to your burden.'

'Look,' Lauren pointed out agitatedly, 'if I'm to be the master chef, what will all these other people be doing?'

'Precisely what you tell them to do. I presume you'll float around with a spoon in your hand saying, "Stir that," or, "Fry this." They'll get the hang of it.'

'It's not them I'm worrying about. To begin with I'll do everything myself. You can get me a person to wash dishes. When is the first conference or whatever?'

'Hold it!' Ryan held up his hand and stood upright. 'Lunch, a walk on the beach and then talk. You can settle in here before you start this new career.'

But she was not settled, not in any way. There were two servants in the house, both of Mexican origin, Lauren guessed, and one of them came now to announce lunch. Lauren would rather have had a sleep because they had been travelling for ages but Ryan didn't seem to need sleep. Now that they were here, he looked more alert and physically perfect than ever. She hoped she would be able to keep up with him.

Lunch made her even more sleepy but she wouldn't have missed the walk on the beach. The wind blew in her hair and she could feel the heat touching her face.

'I'll get as brown as you.' She smiled up at Ryan and his glance slid over her perfect skin.

'Don't try it. You're too fair. A little at a time until you're used to it.'

'Please don't patronise me, Ryan.' His tone had taken the pleasure out of things. They were not talking as equals. He was the big boss.

'Am I doing that? I really thought I was looking after you.'

'I don't need looking after. I can manage very well by myself.'

'Can you? All right, Lauren. From now on we'll assume that you can. Let's go back. We have tomorrow to discuss.'

He turned round abruptly and Lauren had no alternative but to follow him. His pace tired her too and she found herself almost jogging to keep up with him. She had offended him, and why? Because he still wanted to look after her as if she were a child.

'You should get married and have children of your own,' she said angrily.

'I intend to.' He never bothered to turn round.

'Well, whoever she is, get on with it,' Lauren snapped. 'Maybe then you'll stop treating me like a child.'

He stopped and waited for her, his gaze running over her sceptically.

'Am I treating you like a child? I'll have to stop at once. As to my future bride, I haven't told her yet.'

'Oh, you're so arrogant!' Lauren stormed. 'Surely you've made a mistake there? You don't tell a woman to marry you, you ask her—if you're normal!'

'I'm perfectly normal,' he assured her wryly. 'The lady in question has the problem. She's not normal at all.'

'You're marrying a moron?' Lauren enquired waspishly.

'Of course not. By the time I marry her she'll be cured.' He stood laughing down at her and she felt exhausted with frustration. He could certainly wind her up!

'You're tired,' he said mockingly. 'Better have a little nap. Tonight I'm taking you out.'

'I don't want to go out! I'm exhausted!' Lauren felt as if she couldn't take one more step and Ryan swung her up into his arms.

'Exhaustion is not allowed. You're in California. We live every minute to the full.'

'Is there a high death-rate?' Lauren asked tiredly. If he enjoyed himself at this pace, what sort of work would he expect? She never asked to be put down either. She was grateful not to have to walk back.

'No worries,' he said easily. 'I'm looking after you.'

'That's what's worrying me,' Lauren murmured, and fell fast asleep.

She found out next day exactly why Ryan had changed. The main offices of the Landis Group were situated in the middle of the city and it had taken a long drive to get there.

'Why do you live so far away from work?' she asked as they negotiated the traffic.

'I don't. In normal circumstances I spend the week in my apartment here. The house is for weekends and holidays, for the rare moments when I have nothing to do.'

'Well, don't think you have to live there because I do now,' Lauren remarked quietly. This morning she was nervous and it wasn't just the new job, the over-whelming sight of the city. It was Ryan. His amused mockery was gone. She might well have just met him. The hard power was right on the surface and it had been there since she had seen him at breakfast.

'I can't live there,' he murmured absently. 'When you're settled you'll be on your own. I can give you two weeks at the most—providing nothing comes up that demands my immediate attention. After that, you manage all by yourself.'

It had an ominous ring and Lauren glanced at him anxiously but the lean handsome profile was perfectly still and aloof, his attention on the road. The car phone rang and he lifted it impatiently.

'Landis.' The clipped tone said everything she had been feeling. She was here with a stranger—her new boss. 'I'm on my way,' he said. 'Set it up ready, Jill.'

Lauren wondered who Jill was. She was probably one of a dozen secretaries, all glamorous. Lauren had never felt so unprepared for anything in her life.

The offices added to her feeling of being out of her depth. Towering skywards, gleaming glass and steel with the one name—Landis—in high blue lettering that looked intimidating. The car swept to the front of the building and a uniformed young man sprang out from nowhere to drive it away, his greeting of Ryan the nearest Lauren had seen to a salute.

Ryan nodded rather grimly and then she was hurrying across a huge foyer, trying to keep up with Ryan's long, easy strides and determined not to fall one pace behind like a servant.

'Could you perhaps give me a head start?' she asked crossly and Ryan looked down at her in surprise, the old sardonic expression back on his face.

'I can't carry you everywhere, honey. It would spoil your image. You're here to make an impression as a forceful businesswoman who is taking on the Landis Group.'

'I don't require transport,' Lauren snapped, blushing at his derision. 'I merely want a more reasonable pace.

I don't happen to be six feet two and I have to take a stride and a half to one of yours.'

'Here's the elevator,' he pointed out. 'You'll get your breath back.'

'It's a lift,' Lauren muttered, glaring at him. 'Don't think I'm changing at all.'

'Your accent will be an advantage,' Ryan said drily. 'It will add a certain touch of something to the lunches. I'll watch with keen interest.'

He was goading again, she noted, but there was a lack of warmth that made her feel completely out on her own. It no longer felt quite so safe and she could not really imagine herself rushing to him in a panic if things went wrong. She could see without anything being pointed out that Ryan was a tough, aloof tycoon and why he had spared the time to go to England and interfere in her life she couldn't think.

There was a lot of springing to attention as they came out near the top floor of the building. For all the hush of luxury there was a great deal of scurrying to and fro and she could tell that this had been going on long before they arrived. It probably never stopped. Ryan just sailed through and Lauren went with him, feeling most definitely superfluous to requirements.

In a huge suite of rooms at the furthest point of the floor, Ryan finally went to ground. It seemed to Lauren that she had not been the only one trotting behind him. He now had a whole sheaf of papers in his hand, thrust there by busy-looking assistants who had waylaid him on the way to his private office.

They walked into a very splendid outer office and a woman looked up from the desk, smiling and standing when she saw Ryan.

'I've set it up for ten-thirty,' she informed him. 'Most people were already on their way. It is the monthly review time after all.'

'Good.' Ryan just grunted at her and dropped the papers on her desk. 'Go through these and let me have them sorted into some order of priority.' They followed him through to his office and he suddenly glanced at Lauren as if he had just noticed she was there. 'This is Lauren Moore, Jill,' he introduced. 'She'll be there this morning. After that she'll be around most of the time— well, every time she's needed.'

Jill wasn't exactly what Lauren had expected. For a start she was about fifty, smart and well-groomed but anything other than glamorous. Her dark hair was cut in a short bob, her suit smart and neat. The perfect secretary but most definitely not what Lauren had imagined.

'My right-hand man,' Ryan said, nodding in Jill's direction. 'Jill thinks for me.'

'It's never necessary.' Jill smiled at Lauren and shook hands. 'Are you...is she...?'

'Another secretary?' Ryan enquired, his attention on something else entirely. 'Lauren is our new secret weapon, Jill. She's going to feed the people who attend the meetings and get them back on the job in double-quick time.'

'Oh!' Jill looked somewhat dumbfounded and Ryan shot her an amused look.

'Think she's too beautiful to cook?' he drawled. 'She's a very talented lady.'

'I'm hoping to be able to cope,' Lauren said firmly, speaking for the first time, and Jill's astounded looks melted into smiles.

'Oh, English!' she said happily, evidently glad about it.

'I'm her guardian,' Ryan announced.

'I'm his stepsister!' Lauren corrected, glaring at him.

'My burden,' Ryan asserted, ignoring both of them and picking up the phone which had begun to ring. To Lauren's chagrin he snapped his fingers and motioned her to the door, dismissing her as if she were a slave. Jill took her arm and drew her out into the other office.

'If you're a relative you'll obviously know he's teasing,' she said soothingly, her lips twitching at the look on Lauren's face.

'I'm not a relative and I may very well kill him and go back home,' Lauren said threateningly. 'He's impossible.'

'Oh, no,' Jill protested. 'He's in a great mood today. He's probably pleased to have you with him. Just wait until somebody makes a mess of things and then see how he is. We all duck. He never raises his voice but those eyes——' she shuddered '—they go all hard green and cold and he can kill at a distance with no words necessary.'

'Then I probably *will* go home,' Lauren assured her.

'Let's have a coffee,' Jill laughed. 'I'm sure he won't ever be annoyed with you.'

Not much! She would probably be the first to feel the wrath. At any rate, it looked as if she might have an ally here. She liked Jill. At the moment she certainly didn't like Ryan and he would not like her one little bit if she made a mess of things.

Jill phoned through to warn Ryan as ten-thirty approached and Lauren's lips tightened. She had been sitting here for ages waiting. Here was where she sat around further and waited. She wasn't even sure what she was waiting for; Ryan had stayed in his office and ignored her. Now there was a meeting. She had visions of him leaving her here all day and collecting her when it was time to go home. Jill must feel as if she was minding the dog!

He appeared, signalling to her imperiously, every inch the tycoon. He hardly even glanced at her and Lauren stayed right where she was. Jill had needed no signal. As his door opened she was on her feet, notebook at the ready and a smile on her face that actually looked genuine.

'This way, Lauren.' Ryan stopped on his way to the door to wait for her, evidently surprised that she hadn't scurried after him, and it wiped the grim look from her face.

'Me? I—I thought you had a meeting.'

'*We* have a meeting,' he assured her. 'You can come with me and sit in on things. Look at the sort of people they are and plan to feed them. This meeting will be fairly short and there are only a dozen people but it will give you some idea.'

Jill had gone off in front and Lauren felt a slight rise in panic.

'But—but won't they object? I—I mean ... I'll be sitting there and listening. It's a private meeting and....'

'It's *my* meeting! Nobody will object. Unless you plan to make this a business venture and strike out on your own, you're working for me. That being the case, you go where I want you to go.'

Normally his tone would have brought forth a resentful comment from her but Lauren was quite tongue-tied and filled with the certain knowledge that she was walking on very thin ice. There was a definite sensation of having burned her boats in coming with Ryan and he was nothing at all as she had imagined. The impression she had had on seeing him again in England was all too real. He was no longer her childhood friend and protector. He was terribly changed.

'If you plan to make a speech, please begin, I'm in a hurry,' he said in a briskly impatient voice when she just stood and stared at him solemnly.

'Oh—er—no. I was just dreaming ...'

He slanted her a wry look, his dark brows raised quizzically. 'Really? You pick the strangest times. Try to gather your thoughts together. You have some serious planning to do. This is the one and only dry run you get. After this, I expect to be fed, expertly and in a very short time. This way.'

He politely indicated the door and Lauren hurried forward a trifle red-faced, quite realising that she had just been reprimanded by the chairman of the board. She was no longer escaping from irascible employers. One of them had captured her and it was a situation from which she could not resign.

CHAPTER SIX

THEY went by lift to the top floor and here the luxury was more pronounced.

'The suite of rooms here consists of a small and a larger boardroom,' Ryan informed her. 'Today we're using the smaller one but Jill will show you around before we leave. There are a couple of other rooms on this floor that might be useful to you. However, I'll deal with all that later. We're in here.'

Lauren just had time to check her appearance in a mirror and then she was being ushered into a room that seemed enormous to her. There was an instant silence as Ryan walked in and then a faint murmur of sound that she knew was surprise. They had not expected an onlooker and many pairs of male eyes regarded her with interest.

They were seated around a great, long mahogany table, every head turned in her direction. Jill was already seated at the end of the table in a chair set slightly back from the one that was obviously for Ryan. Everyone got slowly to their feet as Lauren came in and their politeness embarrassed her further.

'You can sit over there,' Ryan murmured indifferently, indicating a leather upholstered chair that stood to the side of the room. As far as she could see it would give everyone a further chance to stare at her as if she were some contestant in a Best Brain of the Year show. It was normally something that she would have ignored but as she was feeling extremely vulnerable at the moment it added to her anxiety and brought out her worst fault—the ability to snap.

'I'll feel like the cat,' she whispered crossly. 'Surely there's a basket?' Ryan spun round and pinned her with green eyes, his broad shoulders sheltering her momentarily.

'Don't talk yourself into trouble,' he warned quietly. 'I'm prepared to ease you in gently. I'm also prepared to pick you up and shake you.'

Lauren didn't try arguing. It had been stupidity anyway. It was just that all her sophistication seemed to have deserted her and she badly wanted Ryan to keep her close to him and reassure her. It was time to pull herself together and she walked to the chair and sat down gracefully, smiling into the sea of faces that were still turned in her direction. They all looked very pleased with themselves and Ryan gave her an extremely derisive glance before taking his place at the head of the table.

'Lauren Moore, gentlemen,' he introduced. 'You'll get to know her after a while. She's not here to listen to the meeting but rather to observe you all very carefully. I'll explain things later.'

It brought about a great straightening of ties and Lauren got a few wary looks. She wondered who they thought she was. At least it relaxed her, because, to some extent, the boot was on the other foot. The observers now felt insecure. She wanted to laugh suddenly. Ryan was unique. One rather menacing sentence and he had thrown them into a minor panic. Small wonder he made millions grow.

She saw a slight smile edging Jill's lips. No doubt she had seen him in action plenty of times. Everyone looked hastily away as if Lauren was about to point to one of them and make some dreadful comment. They left her in peace and Ryan got right down to the meeting with no further lingering. He had cut her right out of his mind and Lauren looked at him curiously, able to observe him as well as everyone else.

How strange to recognise somebody and yet not know them at all. This was her dearest Ryan, who had cared for her, protected her, loved her. He knew all her youthful secrets, had guided her through her childhood, and yet she didn't know him now.

It was the same handsome face, the same dark hair, the same astonishing eyes that could turn from brilliant green to olive darkness, cat-like eyes that often seemed to light up inside. The same strong, graceful hands were moving now, stressing some point. They were the hands that had mended her bicycle, made her swing, corrected her tennis shots but when they touched her now she felt strange.

She was not aware of anything that was being said and they were all too intent on Ryan to even notice her. There was a flurry of papers as people consulted their notes and Ryan glanced up, his eyes meeting hers and sweeping over her face. For a second she couldn't look away, unaware that she too was searching his face for something that seemed to have gone with the lost years. Again there was this desperate yearning to grasp the past, but it was gone.

Ryan looked away abruptly as someone spoke and Lauren got down to business, shaking off the sudden melancholy, reminding herself that this was the only dry run. What would they like to eat? They all seemed to be successful, well-dressed businessmen who were quite used to dining out at good places. Feed them well but don't over-feed them. Back to work on the gong with enough energy left to achieve something realistic. Those were basically Ryan's orders.

She pursed her lips, her dark eyes narrowing, her head on one side. It was time she settled down to this new job and she had every intention of enjoying it. Maybe she would eventually strike out on her own. What would Ryan say then? There was a lot of planning to do but suddenly she felt able to manage. It was very exciting and one of the things that made it so was because she was stepping into Ryan's world, a world she didn't know at all.

At the end of the meeting, the men who had watched her with interest as she came in seemed now only intent on escape as if she would capture them and ask embarrassing questions in a loud voice. It was all greatly amusing and her amusement showed on her face as her eyes met Ryan's. His own eyes narrowed in complete understanding and she got that tilted smile that was really no more than a quirk of the lips but which spoke volumes. He had never needed to have things spelled out to him. He always *knew*.

Two of the men stayed behind and Ryan brought them to meet her.

'These are the only two you'll need to know well, Lauren,' he assured her. 'They both work closely with me.'

Even these two looked a trifle uneasy and she knew that Ryan had in no way enlightened them. One of the men was young, a good-looking man with fair hair and an assurance about him that spelled success. Ryan introduced him as Shaw Newark. He seemed to be about thirty. He was tall and well-dressed, not so tall as Ryan but quite an impressive man even though most people faded into insignificance beside the boss.

'Shaw is a lawyer,' Ryan explained. 'He manages our affairs and points out anything I can't do.'

'I try,' Shaw said drily. 'My remarks are noted and often ignored. If I want Ryan, I normally have to run after him.'

'Who doesn't?' The other man joined in the conversation and from the look on his face, even from his

general attitude, Lauren could see that here was a man
that Ryan liked. His name was Jim Sheldon and he was
a sharp contrast to Shaw Newark. Jim was a short man,
merry-faced and rapidly moving from stocky to over-
weight. He looked as if he loved being alive and he was
older than either Ryan or Shaw.

'Jim does the books,' Ryan said with a grin. 'He *really*
frightens me.'

'Accountant, greatly harassed,' Jim assured her,
shaking her hand. 'Ryan is about to explain your mysterious arrival.'

'Over lunch?' Shaw asked, looking at Lauren with
speculative eyes.

'Why not?' Ryan took Lauren's arm and began to
move to the door. 'I warn you, though, it had better be
good. You're in the company of an expert.'

They both looked completely mystified and Ryan regarded Lauren intently for a moment before adding,
'Lauren is taking over the catering for the Landis Group.
As from today, she's on the payroll. She's here to lighten
my burden and remove all my irritation.' Obviously he
had noticed the determination on her face and knew she
would see it through.

'If she can do that last she's worth every cent,' Jim
said cheerfully and Shaw looked at her closely.

'I don't think this beautiful lady runs to cents,' he
murmured admiringly, his eyes on her glowing skin and
shining hair, her expensive clothes. 'Where did you find
her?' he added, speaking to Ryan but never taking his
eyes from Lauren.

'I didn't have to find her. I've always known exactly
where she was,' Ryan said very softly. 'Lauren is my
stepsister.' He left them for a minute to speak to Jill and
Shaw looked slightly embarrassed.

'Why do I get the feeling that the tiger just shook
me?' he murmured worriedly.

'That indefinable air of silken menace. You should know it by now,' Jim pointed out drily. 'When you've been with Ryan as long as I have you'll learn that safety follows caution—lots of caution.'

'But nobody did anything wrong,' Lauren protested. 'He's not so frightening surely?'

'Normally, no,' Jim agreed, glancing at her in amusement. 'Let's just say, though, that if anyone steps on the tiger's tail it had better be you. We'll just watch, then we'll duck fast.'

When Ryan joined them she couldn't see any sign of temper on his face and the meal at a nearby restaurant was very enjoyable. Whatever had scared Shaw, he was now back to normal and entertained her whole-heartedly without getting any icy green looks from Ryan. They were interested in the whole project and, as the accountant, Jim was all for it.

By the time they left for home, Lauren felt she had at least managed to get her foot in the door. While Ryan was busy after lunch, Jill showed Lauren round the building. It was most impressive, especially a rather secret-looking lift that captured Lauren's attention.

'What's that?' she enquired.

'*That* is private,' Jill informed her firmly, 'although I don't expect it's private to you. It leads up to Ryan's apartment.'

'Up? I thought this was the top floor?' They were in the bigger of the two boardrooms and there was the definite impression that they were at the top of the building. The street seemed to be miles below.

'Optical illusion,' Jill laughed. 'Above this is the penthouse, Ryan's lair. We all have the worrying feeling that he controls the world from there. Nobody goes there,' she added in a dark, dramatic voice. 'Tell me what it's like.'

'I'll wheedle my way in,' Lauren promised with a grin. 'First, though, I'll have to be good at my job and well behaved; I can't always manage that last bit.'

'A fight with Ryan!' Jill shuddered. 'Too terrible to contemplate. The only person who ever raises his voice to Ryan is Jim Sheldon.'

'Jim?' Lauren looked at her in amazement, not able to believe it.

'Oh, Jim can be bold and daring,' Jill said with a smile, adding, 'In any case, Ryan likes him. You'll probably see a lot of Jim and Alice Sheldon. They're a well-matched couple and very close to Ryan's heart. They're often down at his beach house. Where are you staying, but the way?'

'At the house.' It suddenly seemed a bit outrageous, even if she had been practically raised by Ryan, and Lauren felt her face flush.

'Ah!' Jill turned to the door. 'Well, that's the grand tour over, Lauren. Have you decided where you're going to work?'

'Somewhere up here,' Lauren murmured, 'if Ryan approves. I'll talk it over with him when we . . . have time.' She had been about to say 'when we get home' but she stifled the words. She felt uneasy. It worried her that she was with Ryan at the house and she couldn't think of any good reason why it should. The knowledge had surprised Jill, she was sure of that.

She tried to shake off the feeling but it clung insidiously and after the unusual day she found herself looking at Ryan stealthily on the way home. He was a bit too magnificent to be the Ryan she knew. She wondered how she had dared to speak to him as she had when he had first come back to England. Now there was the feeling that she should watch her step and she didn't know if it was other people's great awe of him or if it was coming from inside her.

When he glanced across she hastily looked out of the car window and she might have known that she wouldn't get away with that.

'Let's have it,' he ordered. 'Whatever's on your mind, now is the time to confess.'

'There's nothing to confess about,' Lauren assured him quickly. 'I haven't had the time to get into mischief today.'

'Stop hiding!' he ordered sharply, not amused. 'I know these wicked-child expressions, so abandon them, they no longer work. Thoughts are racing around in that peculiar head of yours and as I'm likely to be the one to pick up the pieces I claim the right to know before the rest of the world.'

'It's about living with you,' Lauren blurted out a little anxiously.

'Rephrase, please!' He shot her a quite cold look and icy though it was it brought a quick flush to her face.

'About staying at your house,' Lauren corrected nervously. 'It probably looks bad. It didn't go down too well with Jill...I think.' She seemed to have talked herself into a hole and she would have dearly liked to avoid it. It was too late now.

'And she said?' Ryan clipped out at her.

'She said, "Ah!"'

Ryan shot her a wryly surprised look and then concentrated on his driving. They were getting close. She assumed that because she could see the sea all the time. The highway ran close to it, sometimes almost on the shoreline and sometimes above it on spectacular cliffs. It was beautiful, lifting the spirits.

'So where do you want to live, Laurie?' Ryan asked quietly and it gave her a wonderful feeling. It was years since he had called her that. He was the only one who ever did.

'I—I love the house by the beach,' she confessed, glancing at him anxiously, wanting to kick herself for ever bringing this up. After all, it was sheer nonsense. It was all due to this feeling of being at the side of Ryan and not part of him as she had felt all her life. It was because he had become a rather powerful stranger who filled her with a certain amount of awe.

'But you don't want me in it with you,' he concluded and she shot round in her seat to stare at him in near-horror.

'I never said that! I never even thought it! I'm not sure how I'd manage without you near. Anyway, it's your house and—and ...'

'I told you that I'd be in my apartment soon enough,' he reminded her quietly and contrarily she didn't like that either.

'The penthouse. I know,' she muttered glumly.

To her relief he suddenly laughed, shooting a glance of sheer amusement at her.

'What do you want? You want a swap? Me to the beach house, you to the penthouse?'

'Heavens, no!' Lauren said quickly. 'Jill says that nobody ever goes up there.'

'We'll make an exception with you,' he promised, still grinning to himself. 'I can see that as usual this conversation has got us exactly nowhere. Now do you think you could stop treating me with such a great amount of anxiety? I can't imagine what's brought it about.'

'I've seen you in action,' Lauren pointed out, although it was not that at all, as she well knew. 'Shaw said he felt as if a tiger had given him a shaking.'

'Not yet,' Ryan assured her quietly.

They had arrived and he turned the car down the road that led to the beach, running it into the garage beneath the house and coming round to help her out before she could move.

'Isn't it beautiful?' Lauren said softly, looking out to sea. The sun was glittering across the water, dazzling, its light catching the windows of the house as they climbed the steps to the veranda.

'It is,' Ryan agreed quietly. 'I always promised myself that one day I would just sit here and watch the sea for hours, do nothing else.'

'Haven't you done that yet?' Lauren glanced at him curiously. There was a certain weariness to his voice that was not tiredness. Each day she discovered a new part to Ryan, she who had thought she knew him so well.

'I've never felt tranquil enough. To just sit like that you have to be completely happy.'

'And you're not?'

'Not yet. Perhaps one day.' He gave her one of his tilted enigmatic smiles and suddenly she wanted to run to him and throw her arms around him because when he looked like that he was further away from her than ever.

'I want to stay here with you,' she said firmly, caution cast to the winds.

'And everybody else can go damn and take their astonishment with them?'

'As far as I'm concerned,' she assured him, tossing her fair head defiantly.

'We'll give it a whirl,' he promised. 'Now if you don't mind I have things to do that just won't wait, and you, my problem child, have a plan to draw up. You can call it "How to succeed brilliantly and save myself from being shaken by a tiger".' He gave her a wide grin and walked off to his study.

Lauren ran up to her luxurious room and threw herself down on the bed for a minute. What did it matter what anyone thought after all? She was exactly where she wanted to be, in this wonderful house by the sea, and she became thoughtful as she admitted that she wanted to be with Ryan too. He was so much a part of her past that she could never give him up gladly and now he was urging her into the future. If she could do well, her life would be very different and, after all, she had wanted it to be different for a long time.

They should convert a room on the same floor as the boardrooms. Lauren put the idea rather worriedly to Ryan but he agreed at once.

'Fine! Right on the job with no waiting. Where do we dish up the goodies?'

'Well, that's a problem,' Lauren mused. They were sitting in the wonderful room that faced the sea, the one with the great glass doors that led to the veranda and Ryan was lying back in a chair as Lauren curled up on the long, cosy settee. 'I haven't thought that out,' she confessed. 'I imagined you'd refuse to alter anything. There's the time factor too. I'm asking to have that room converted into a modern kitchen.'

'Two days,' Ryan assured her, 'well, maybe three, depending on how fussy you are.'

'Two days! I thought it would take ages.'

'Honey, I'm paying for this,' he said drily. 'Any firm who can't work fast can work elsewhere.'

She had terrible visions of people being out of business because of her and he saw her expression.

'Coded Kitchens,' he murmured. 'The Group owns the company.'

'Oh, well. If they work for you they deserve anything that's coming to them,' Lauren said pertly. 'That being the case, what about a dining-room? I think it would be just too pointed to serve them while they were still sitting in the boardroom, don't you?'

Ryan grinned at her and nodded. For a minute he was thoughtful then he said, 'What the hell? Who needs two boardrooms? It's altogether decadent. You can have the small boardroom. You want one big table or a restaurant atmosphere?'

It left Lauren almost open-mouthed. He was willing to turn the whole place upside-down.

'Why are you doing this?' she asked worriedly. 'It's a lot of expense. It will upset things, bring about a certain feeling of being disorganised.'

'It had better not,' Ryan growled. 'I want this up and running before I have to fly off to Canada.'

'When?' Lauren's heart sank one huge notch. He was going away. How would she manage?

'One week from today,' he told her indifferently. 'Let's walk on the beach. I've had enough planning.'

'But I haven't finished! What about furnishings? What about supplies? What about ... ?'

'Walk!' Ryan ordered, pulling her to her feet. 'Tell me exactly what you want and I'll get Jill on to it. The hard fittings will be in place two or three days from now. Your first event will be the day after.'

He stepped out on to the veranda and turned to the steps and this time he didn't need to order her to go with him. She trotted beside him anxiously, filled with misgivings again.

'Four days from now? It's too soon! I'm not at all ready.'

'Then get ready, because when the time comes they'll all be sitting banging their spoons and waiting.'

'Then you'll look a complete fool!' Lauren pointed out stormily.

His arm lashed round her as they stepped to the soft sand and his free hand tilted her chin.

'And how will you look, Miss Moore?' he enquired wryly.

'Desperate,' she confessed, watching him warily and seeing his eyes turn all shades of green like the far reaches

of the sea. One thing was certain, he wasn't annoyed.
There was no clear, icy colour. He was probably teasing.

'When do I really start?' she asked shakily.

'I just told you. If you're going in off the deep end
it's best to get it over with quickly.'

He meant it. She stared up at him wildly and saw the
tilted smile grow to a wide grin, but all the same he meant
it.

'Oh, my goodness,' she whispered, and he began to
laugh softly, his arm still round her as they set off for
their walk. She was glad he held her because she felt like
sinking down and just simply refusing. Talk was over.
Ryan wanted action.

'You'll be fine,' he said quietly, dropping a kiss on
her forehead. She hoped so. She knew that Ryan set high
standards and he was trusting her not to let him down.
She wouldn't either, even if she had to stay up all night
until then.

It seemed to be on her before she could think. She had
spent the days supervising the kitchen and the new
dining-room with hardly a moment to speak to Ryan.
At night he had too much work to do to be more than
faintly sociable and Lauren was too busy working out
menus to care. First one and then another was discarded
and when she finally settled on one she had to find
suppliers.

Jill was a treasure. She seemed to know everything
and as the dreaded day approached Lauren was tensed
up to screaming-point. It was not that she really felt incapable either. It was because she was terrified of letting
Ryan down. She tried all the recipes at home and Maria
helped her. The little Mexican woman was a good cook
in her own right and she was pleased to be in on things.
Her only scowl was when Lauren would have thrown the
finished food away.

'But I don't want Mr Landis to see it,' Lauren pointed out as Maria flatly refused to throw out the beautiful food.

'He will not, Señorita Lauren,' Maria said emphatically. 'Constanza and I—we eat it!'

Well, it was better than wasting it, and that night at dinner Lauren couldn't eat anything at all. She felt she had been tasting food all day.

'Lost your appetite?' Ryan asked.

'Er—I seem to have.' Lauren looked at him cautiously and he lifted his head, sniffing the air.

'There's a wonderful smell of cooking in the house. I'm quite disappointed with dinner,' he mused. 'I thought you'd been trying your hand at things.'

'I have,' Lauren confessed, seeing no way out of it. 'It's tomorrow's lunch.'

'So why aren't I eating it?' he demanded.

'I wanted you to get a surprise tomorrow,' she managed lamely and he gave her a rueful look.

'I'd rather have had a delight tonight. Where is it?'

'Maria and Constanza, they—er—— Well, I was going to throw it away and...'

'It was no good?'

'It was wonderful!' She sat up straight and stared at him balefully until she realised she was being teased again. He was grinning at her.

'See that I get served first tomorrow,' he ordered and she nodded anxiously before saying with a certain amount of desperation, 'Can I have Maria and Constanza? I'd like to take them with me and...'

'Sure. Anything you want. Just slacken off. If I didn't have faith in you I wouldn't be doing this.' His hand covered hers on the table and her fingers tightened involuntarily around his.

'When you're in Canada...' she began rather desperately.

'There'll be no board meetings,' he finished for her. 'You can stay here and perfect a few more delightful dishes.'

'Oh!' She suddenly felt safe again and her tight body relaxed. Ryan kept hold of her hand, turning it in his, looking down at her slender fingers.

'I won't let you sink, Laurie,' he said softly. 'Don't rely on me too much, though. I can't always be here.'

'I know,' she said quickly. 'I'll not cling to you. I promise. I'll start to lead my own life soon enough and let you get on with yours.'

'Well, thank you,' he said drily and she flushed as his sardonic eyes looked up into hers. It made her blurt out something she had been going to put a little more diplomatically.

'Shaw wants me to go out with him. He wants to take me to a nightclub. I thought I might go when you're in Canada.'

'Why not? He's a regular flier. You don't have to ask me.' He sat back and drank his wine and Lauren felt quite foolish.

'I wasn't asking you,' she said sharply. 'As I'm staying here I thought it only courteous to tell you. In any case, it was just conversation.'

'Well, well. Another stage of understanding reached,' he drawled derisively and she felt quite miserable.

'Do you want to walk on the beach?' she asked anxiously. 'It's bright moonlight.'

'Too busy. I'll see you in the morning.' Before she could think of anything else to say he had nodded to her politely and walked out of the room and Lauren bit her lip in vexation. Now what had she done? She knew how Shaw had felt at that meeting. The tiger had managed to shake her too and all for nothing as far as she could see. This food had better be good or he would savage her.

Next morning Ryan was particularly silent and Lauren looked at him a little resentfully. It was her big day. He might have been a bit more friendly. Maria and Constanza were sitting proudly in the back of the car, surrounded by dozens of things that Lauren had decided to bring at the last minute.

She kept quiet herself. She had one bit of planning that Ryan didn't know about and she wondered how it would go down. Well, today was the day. If it failed she would be at a loose end and probably get that good shaking. Not that it would fail, she assured herself hastily. The kitchen was stocked, everything was there and she knew exactly what she was doing.

As they walked into the building she found herself almost frog-marching her two assistants forward. They were utterly mesmerised by the splendour and Lauren urged them to the lift quickly.

'Good luck,' Ryan called out to her as she hurried away, and all she could manage was a rather tight smile. She wasn't sure if he even noticed that. He was already being accosted by busy-looking members of his staff. She was on her own.

He rang her just as she had arrived at her floor.

'Last-minute adjustment,' he said laconically. 'You'll have twenty.'

'People?' Her face fell. She had expected the same twelve.

'We only feed people,' he murmured sardonically. 'Can you cope?'

'I can!' She had the decided feeling that this was some sort of trick, that he had known all along and not enlightened her. Therefore, it was very necessary to get the better of him. She slammed the phone down.

Jill rang ten minutes later, full of apologies.

'Lauren, I'm sorry about the numbers. I got it all mixed up the other day. I only told Ryan as he walked in this morning. He looked very cross. I hope you're not?'

'I'll manage,' Lauren said breezily. 'Numbers don't matter as we have plenty of supplies.' She had her fingers crossed. Numbers mattered very much indeed, especially as they were almost doubled. Well, it wasn't Ryan's fault after all. She gave one anxious glance at the clock and went into furious action, driving her two assistants before her like a well-established tyrant. Nothing must go wrong.

Her surprise proved to be spectacular. Maria and Constanza had brought their much prized Mexican dresses, cream cotton with swirling skirts brightly patterned at the hems. They had flowers in their hair, thonged sandals on their feet and, as the meeting split up and the board members joined the others in the newly furbished dining-room, Maria and Constanza swept in with bright smiles to serves drinks.

Lauren did a little peeking without being seen. It seemed to be going down well but she couldn't see Ryan. She wasn't sure how he would take it. She was determined to keep out of sight. With the meal ready to serve she had changed into a silk shift, a dress of sage-green, a colour that enhanced the thick golden necklace she wore. Her hair was swept up quite severely, a style that showed off her astonishing fairness. If she had to go in there at least she would look good. It boosted her ego and steadied her nerves.

She noticed there were a few women here today and by the way they were talking she knew they were not wives but high-powered members of the Landis Group. Did they dare stand up and contradict Ryan? How did he take it? She tore herself away from her vantage-point and cast her eyes expertly around the preparations.

The starters—seafood cocktails—were already on the tables. It would give the three of them a breathing space before the main course, which was veal scaloppine *à la creme* with rice. She heard Ryan's dark voice suggesting that everyone begin and Maria and Constanza came sailing back in, bright-faced and proud. So far, so good. Lauren grimaced as she realised she would not have been one bit nervous had it not been for Ryan's presence. She loved doing this.

She had planned to remain out of sight all the time but as the meal drew to a close, the strawberry tartlets eaten and the coffee prepared, Lauren decided it was time to make an appearance. She had to take a deep breath. For years she had been quite sure of herself but she was very nervous now. For one thing she had the odd feeling of not knowing exactly who she was. She felt in a sort of limbo between being closely linked with Ryan and being merely a very lowly employee.

The coffee was to be served at a side-table in the room and as Lauren opened the door to go in there she was well aware that nobody here would bother her. It was the thought of those scathing green eyes on her that brought about any sort of nervousness at all. She lifted her head proudly and walked in, ignoring everyone. She was here to do a job and nothing more.

There was too much talk for her to be really noticed and as Lauren stood at the flower-bedecked table and began to serve the coffee Shaw stood and came towards her. It seemed to be the signal for others to mingle and discuss things and that was a good deal better than being stared at.

'Superb!' Shaw came for his coffee and smiled at her admiringly. 'I doubt if there's anything left on even one plate.'

'I'm glad,' Lauren laughed. 'Ryan's idea of keeping them all in the building has to pay off or I'm fired.'

'What would you do then?' Shaw regarded her with deep interest but she had no time to think of some amusing quip—Ryan answered for her and she hadn't even seen him approach.

'Just stay with me, lie on the beach and get brown. I was almost hoping for a fiasco. Sometimes I think she's too beautiful to work.'

He took his coffee and wandered away and Lauren stared after him thoughtfully. There was no knowing what he meant. He hadn't congratulated her, he hadn't even looked too pleased.

'I wonder if he meant that?' Shaw mused softly, his eyes too on Ryan.

'Not after he's had these rooms converted for me,' Lauren assured him swiftly. 'Ryan doesn't do things for nothing.' In fact she felt quite shaken both by the words and by the look he had given her, an all-encompassing look that had started at her head and moved over her minutely.

'He doesn't say things for nothing either,' Shaw murmured. He glanced keenly at Lauren. 'I'm not stepping on his toes wanting to take you out, am I?'

'How ridiculous!' She felt her face flushing. It *was* ridiculous after all, but there was something about Ryan nowadays that she couldn't understand. He seemed to have gathered her in very closely and she was not a child now, as he had pointed out regularly.

CHAPTER SEVEN

JUST as Lauren thought he was going to ignore her and treat her like the caterer, he reappeared and took her arm, moving her away from Shaw and towards the others, who were deeply in conversation, standing about with their coffee and evidently quite satisfied with things.

'Come and collect a few compliments,' he said softly.

'Sure you don't mean complaints?' Lauren glanced at his handsome profile and he slanted her a goading look.

'You're grieving because I didn't rush up and praise you? I was saving it until we got home.'

'I don't need praise,' Lauren snapped. 'I know good food when I see it. Just pay me and we'll call it square.' In fact she was smarting under the sarcasm. She *had* wanted praise from Ryan and he clearly knew it.

'Don't fight in public, sweetie,' he warned. 'We present a united front to outsiders. Isn't that what we've always done?'

She didn't have the opportunity to take him up on that because he suddenly introduced her in a crisp voice that stopped the talking and then she was on her own, grateful that Jim Sheldon joined her because Ryan deserted her as swiftly as he had captured her and Shaw stayed clear. Maybe he had felt the tiger close again?

'So you're the mysterious relation that Ryan has been keeping hidden?'

The drawling voice brought Lauren's head round sharply and she found herself looking into blue eyes that were certainly not friendly.

'I haven't been hidden. I've been too busy getting ready to work since I came here.' The woman was tall and glamorous, her expensive suit moulded to a good figure. She had thick dark hair that was glossy and beautifully groomed and Lauren took an instant dislike to her. This was one of the powerful women who worked with Ryan and this particular one looked as if she would crush any opposition.

'He told me he'd brought you over from England. You're his half-sister, I hear?'

'His stepsister,' Lauren corrected sweetly. 'No relation at all except by long association.' She had no idea why she said it. Normally she proudly called Ryan a relative even though he wasn't but now she just found the words falling from her lips in a sort of self-defence.

'How odd that he never told me. I'm Janice Powers by the way. Ryan and I—well, we go back a long time, if you see what I mean.'

'Oh, I do,' Lauren muttered, edging away. 'I suppose I should circulate.' It was a lame excuse for just walking off but she felt quite threatened. Claws were extended there. Of course, Ryan would be able to handle a woman like that but Janice Powers left Lauren feeling uneasy. She had felt it necessary to stake a claim on Ryan and had not hesitated at all. Lauren made a rush for Jim and tagged on to him until the others seemed to pick up some unspoken signal from Ryan and drifted out.

It had been a success, so why did she feel let down and miserable? When they had the place to themselves, Maria and Constanza went into action clearing up and Lauren helped. It took her mind off things, things being Ryan's inexplicable hostility to Shaw and Janice Powers's obvious hostility to her. Next time, she would not make an appearance. This high-flying boardroom bit was out of her league.

He took them all home when the time came and
Lauren sat quietly. The stress had quite tired her out and
it was something she would have to get used to. She was
all set to escape to her room and forget it all but Ryan
had other ideas.

'Come in here,' he ordered quietly as Maria and
Constanza rushed happily away. He indicated his study
and Lauren went very reluctantly, her heart beginning
to pound. Now what was he going to say? This feeling
of anxiety with him quite irritated her. If he was going
to play the chairman of the board...

'You look tired,' he said. On top of her anxieties it
annoyed her.

'Jaded and worn out? I'm sorry I can't be quite like
Miss Powers but I'm just an ordinary person.
Superwoman isn't within my scope.'

'I said tired,' Ryan pointed out softly. 'You produced
a meal for all those people with only the amateur help
of Maria and Constanza.'

'I managed. I'm comfortable with them,' Lauren
muttered defensively.

'I want you to be the boss-lady, not the kitchen maid.
I know I dropped the extra people on you suddenly
but...'

'It wasn't your fault. Jill confessed and apologised.
Anyway, I managed.'

'Beautifully. I doubt they'll want any dinner tonight.'

'You mean I overfed them?'

'I mean that other food will taste like cardboard after
that. Why this desire to battle?' He walked across to
where she stood leaning against his desk rather defiantly. 'What exactly is it that ruffled your feathers?'
He planted himself in front of her and fixed her with
those incredible eyes and Lauren ducked her head. It
seemed wise.

'As you pointed out, I'm tired.'

'Janice irritated you? She's a rather compelling female.'

'Impressive. I hardly had time to notice her. She certainly didn't irritate me. She seemed to want to know exactly what our relationship was.'

'Do we have one?' Ryan was watching her with amused green eyes and she flushed, angry that she had put a foot wrong with him.

'She thought I was your half-sister. I corrected her. Now if there's nothing else I'll get changed.'

'There is something else,' he assured her. 'Changes are what I want to speak about. There are no further meetings until I come back from Canada. After that, the meetings will be thick and fast. I want you to have a small and efficient staff by then. We've got to talk about it.'

While he was speaking his hand had begun to take the pins out of her hair. His manner was almost absent-minded, as if he had no idea he was doing it, and Lauren felt as if she was holding her breath, her dark eyes on his thoughtful face.

'I—I'm happy with the two people I've got.' She couldn't understand this sudden need to whisper the words and Ryan didn't seem to notice.

'You want somebody who'll be there before you arrive, somebody who will take orders and not have to be constantly supervised. Go on as you did today and you'll wear yourself out. I never did want a cook. I want you to show somebody how to do things and supervise them.'

He had dropped the pins on his desk and now her hair fell heavily to her shoulders, its shimmering fairness swirling around her face.

'I'll feel uncomfortable. I'm not cut out to be a boss.'

'All you have to do is alter your way of thinking. You'll get used to the idea.'

'Well, I'm not going to,' Lauren said with shaky defiance. 'If you want a bossy female, get Miss Powers to do it.' He was making her feel strange and she was trying to fight her way out of it. Mentioning Janice Powers helped because it annoyed her.

'Janice? I doubt if she could crack an egg successfully.'

'I'm sure she's much too sophisticated. You should know. She said you went back a long way.'

'We do. That's why I know her so well. She's very glossy, don't you think?'

'Plastic-perfect. Can I go now? We've talked about my ability to wear myself out and my determination to stay as I am. I think that about covers it, unless you want to speak further about Miss Powers and her sophistication.'

'Why are you angry?' he asked softly. His fingers suddenly threaded through her hair, running the glittering strands slowly against the light. 'I'm trying to help you.'

'You're trying to change me.' Lauren ducked free and made for the door. 'I want to go on as I did today. Is that too much to ask?'

'And what do I do when you suddenly decide you've had enough? What do I do when you run out on me? I'll have no trained staff.'

Lauren turned and stared at him, her hands clenching angrily. So that was what it was all about; he was covering all possibilities.

'I'm not going to run out on you. Running out on you has nothing to do with this. It's simply my job. You offered it and I'm sticking to it. Just don't try changing me. Concentrate on Janice Powers. I expect she's the one you were telling me about, the one you'll be marrying when you've got her altered to your liking.'

For a moment he looked annoyed but then she got that old enigmatic smile.

'Maybe,' he agreed softly. 'You have to admit she'd be a wonderful asset.'

Lauren never answered. She just didn't want to know, and why she had hammered the point home she couldn't understand. There was this feeling inside her that she hadn't felt since she was eighteen. It was a bitter feeling of being left out, almost jealousy.

She spun round and walked off and Ryan didn't try to stop her although she knew that, once again, their conversation had gone exactly nowhere.

During the night there was a storm. The thunder over the sea woke Lauren and for a minute she lay watching the lightning flash a good way off. Her room had the same great glass doors that the lovely sitting-room had downstairs and she had a balcony that gave a sweeping panoramic view of the Pacific Ocean. It suddenly dawned on her that the window was wide open, the white gauzy curtains being lashed by rain. It was driving this way and soon the carpet would be wet through.

She sprang out of bed and ran across, feeling the chill as she left the warmth of the bed. She had to step right into the blast of the rain to close the window and when she tried it refused to move. Somehow it had become stuck, the sliding mechanism refusing to work at all, and she tugged at it frantically with exactly no result.

It was pointless to try to keep dry. The rain was lashing on to the balcony and straight into the room and the curtains, now hopelessly wet, kept trying to wrap themselves around her. She hammered at the window catches, muttering to herself angrily, but no amount of banging made them move.

Light flooded into the room from the passage and when she turned her head it was to see Ryan striding in and making for her with all speed.

'What the hell are you doing?' he grated, coming up to her and almost flinging her away from the rain.

'They're stuck! This room's going to be flooded. What are we going to do?'

'Close them,' he muttered impatiently. His hand flicked out to a catch she had never even seen and seconds later calm entered the atmosphere as the window slid closed and the rain was vanquished behind the glass.

'I didn't know about that!' Lauren protested as he turned derisive eyes on her. Water seemed to be dripping from her hair and she was shivering.

'Don't you ever experiment?' he wanted to know. 'These are either manual or automatic. That top catch is the automatic one.'

'Maria usually does it and I've never bothered to alter them,' Lauren said lamely, feeling extremely foolish. It was quite dark now and obviously the storm had only just begun. The only light came from the passage and Ryan grunted with exasperation, moving to switch on the lamp by her bed. All the lamps came on and Lauren was then well aware of how bedraggled she looked. A wet rat, a shivering one. Ryan too was slightly wet. He was just in trousers; even his feet were bare and his brown chest was splattered with water.

She never had the time to take action. Ryan strode into her bathroom and came out with a towel, starting at once to rub her hair.

'I wonder what you would have done if I hadn't been awake and heard your hammering and banging?' he muttered. 'Would you have still been at it in the light of day?'

'Of course not!' Lauren managed crossly, escaping from his rather violent ministrations and grabbing the towel herself. 'I would have fathomed it. If I hadn't, I would have called you.' She was furious to have been seen to be incompetent.

'Sooner rather than later, I hope.' He looked tightly annoyed and Lauren glared at him as she rubbed at her hair. It was not necessary to be so stroppy with her. He could have laughed. He *would* have laughed at one time. She told him so heatedly.

'I can't see why you're so annoyed. At one time you would have found this amusing but I suppose now you're too important to have such a great sense of humour. A long time ago you would have laughed. You would have seen the funny side of things.'

'A long time ago,' he agreed tautly. 'I can't see anything funny right now.' His eyes swept over her irritably and it was only then that she realised exactly why she was shivering so much. She was soaked to the skin. Her white satin nightie was clinging to her in just about every place and it might as well have been transparent. She had never given it a thought, any more than she had when Ryan had come to her flat and she had been in pyjamas. She felt completely naked and she gave a small despairing cry, throwing the towel round her shoulders and pulling it close, turning away.

'I—I'm sorry,' she pleaded desperately. 'I never thought... I just jumped up and ran to the window... I...'

'And I just stormed in here with the same old possessiveness,' he said softly.

'Will you go?' Lauren whispered. 'I can't get changed until you go.'

Instead of moving he turned her towards him but she refused to look up. She was too filled with remorse, let alone embarrassment. She always seemed to be getting herself into situations with Ryan.

'Please, Ryan,' she begged shakily and he simply pulled her towards him, folding her in warm arms, her face against his bare chest. It soothed her. Ryan had always been able to soothe her. From guilty embarrassment she was suddenly almost content and she rubbed her face against the slightly abrasive hair on his chest, so grateful to him.

'Thank you.' Lauren looked up with warm, dark eyes. 'I always seem to be making a fool of myself with you nowadays. I feel a lot better now.'

Instead of smiling back and leaving her to get to bed he simply looked down at her, his face still taut.

'I'm glad you feel better,' he said tightly. 'You think I do?' She couldn't speak. There was that peculiar light flaring at the back of his eyes, the brilliant green turned to darkest olive, turbulent and changing even as she looked at him.

'Why—why did you hold me and comfort me if you're still so angry?' she whispered, stricken again, and his hands ran over her damp hair, moulding it to her head, drawing strands of it round her slender neck.

'I was comforting myself,' he corrected thickly. 'It seemed a good idea at the time but now I'm not too sure.' His hold on her tightened. 'I want to finish drying you—all over.'

Lauren couldn't speak. His words hit her like an erotic shock. For a minute she just looked back into his eyes and then she seemed to be moving right into him and she wasn't sure who was doing the moving.

'Ryan!' Just for a second, her hands came to his chest in a forlorn attempt to defend herself but the moment they touched him they seemed to take on a life of their own and as he gathered her close she wound her arms around his neck and went willingly.

There wasn't a single thought in her mind. It was Ryan and it was all right. She murmured his name in bewilderment but his lips caught hers, forcing the words back inside her, and his kiss took her breath away. For the first time in her life she felt liquid heat flood through her. It ran from her head to her feet, melting her inside, dissolving the shivering cold, and her arms tightened around his neck as she turned her mouth up, craving for more.

Ryan groaned and moulded her to him, his mouth moving deeply over hers, and she became more soft and pliant, her fingers sinking into the thick hair at his nape, her mind flying free and wandering far above as his kisses became more hungry. His heart was throbbing heavily over hers, his hands stroking her spine, and Lauren just gave in completely, lost and entranced, knowing how little she had been alive until now, her cool sophistication simply a mask to face the world.

She sagged against him, wanting more of the feelings he was evoking, and Ryan tore his mouth away from hers, his breath ragged in his throat.

'No, honey,' he said unevenly. 'This must stop now.'

Her eyes wouldn't open and her arms still clung to his neck, desperately seeking the magic she had felt, was still feeling.

'Ryan,' she moaned. 'I want...'

'My God, you always did,' he muttered hoarsely. 'Right now, though, you have no choice because I've not left you with one. I've looked after you too long to forget it now.'

She wanted to cry but she didn't. She was too stunned, too bewildered by her own lack of control, and she stood there swaying dizzily as Ryan left her and went for a dry towel. She heard him opening drawers too but nothing really penetrated her entranced mind. She was like someone in a dream.

'Get dry and get into bed.' He came back to her and stood looking down at her, his face tightening when she simply gazed at him, mesmerised. 'All right,' he muttered. 'Why the hell not?'

He stripped the wet nightie from her and wrapped her in the huge towel, his mouth in one straight line of control as she made no move to stop him. It was very obvious that she was completely given up to the heated pleasure that even now coloured her skin, her rapt expression never changing even though his hands were now almost rough as he dried her.

He handed her the dry nightie but she seemed to be too far gone to understand and he whipped the towel away and slid the nightie over her head, drawing her arms through the sleeves and then smoothing her hair while she stood there like a doll.

She looked as if she would stand there all night and he swung her into his arms, stiffening when her lips came instantly to his neck as if she was seeking the fading magic.

'Ryan?' She seemed to come partly out of the trance as he placed her in bed and drew the sheets over her, her eyes seeking his, dark, puzzled, uncomprehending.

He stood over her like a hunter, almost menacing, the tiger again, his eyes brilliantly green in the lamplight.

'I want you,' he said harshly, staring down at her. 'Don't ever forget it again. Next time, I might not remember who you are.'

Lauren watched him stride from the room and then she put out the lamp. It went dark and she stared unseeing into the darkness. Who was she? Ryan's burden, his responsibility, his protégée? She moved restlessly in bed, her limbs still wanting to seek his, and she remembered Ryan's words when he had reminded her that with Kent she would have been making a mistake.

She knew it now and she knew what her mother had meant. What sort of mistake was this, though? She knew that when she came to her senses she would be frightened because, after all, home was far away. She only had Ryan and she was not sure now what he was or who he was. Her dearly loved Ryan was now a dark, vibrant stranger, powerful, determined, and she knew he had saved her from herself tonight. She moaned softly as she realised she had not wanted saving at all.

Lauren slept late. She had been too restless, too bewildered to sleep for ages, and when she finally got up Ryan had already left. It was a relief because she had got ready very slowly, not knowing how to face him. The light of day had made her realise that she had behaved like a fool. Ryan had known it and he had stopped her. That he had started it in the first place never entered her mind. She was only concerned with how she felt inside and it was a sinking, desperate feeling.

She had nothing particularly to do and she found her mind wandering to the future. What now? Could she still stay here with Ryan? Would he want her to find a place of her own? She didn't want to. She loved this house with its views and the constant sound of the sea. She didn't want to be here alone either. She couldn't seem to think of any sort of life with Ryan out of it. The whole thing was madness and no doubt she would come to her senses eventually.

Jill rang at mid-morning and gave her a message.

'Ryan asked me to ring you, Lauren,' she said after they had chatted a few minutes. 'He's staying at his apartment for the rest of the week and then going on to Canada. He says if there's anything you need just ring the store and if you have any trouble ring me.' She would be alone, not even able to go any further than the beach, and Lauren's face fell at this dismissive message.

'Oh, yes,' Jill added. 'There's a car in the garage for you. Ryan says the keys are on his desk in the study. Take care. Remember we drive on the other side of the road.'

'Did Ryan say that?' Lauren asked hopefully but Jill gave an outraged laugh.

'Certainly not! I thought of it all by myself. I have thoughts, you know.'

Lauren sat and surveyed the phone glumly when Jill rang off. She need not have bothered her head about the future. Ryan had taken care of it instantly and ruthlessly. If he had felt a fit of madness last night, he was not going to allow it to happen again. She had no idea when he would be back, how long he would be in Canada. She felt very much alone and when Shaw rang later she was almost desperate to hear a voice she knew. When he asked her out that very evening she leapt at the chance.

If Ryan knew he might disapprove; she had the uneasy feeling that he would. On the other hand he might not know, and, if he did, why shouldn't she go out? Ryan had simply walked off and left her. By the time evening came and she was getting ready she had worked up a silent rage against Ryan that fully encompassed Janice Powers.

She had no doubt how Ryan would be spending his evening and she imagined him in his penthouse suite with the glossy Miss Powers even though she had no idea what it looked like. She had a vivid imagination and it worked at her until she could have screamed with frustration. Once again she had been lulled into thinking of Ryan as her personal possession and once again he had left her in no doubt that he was nothing of the kind.

It was like being eighteen all over again but now she was not a gullible teenager. She knew all about men and desire. Her cheeks flushed when she remembered Ryan bending over her, telling her he wanted her. He had realised she was no longer a child, it seemed. Her lips tightened as she imagined Janice Powers in his arms. She would show him how very much she had changed. If it hadn't dawned on him yet, it would. She was quite capable of making plans and they were not going to include Ryan.

Shaw collected her and drove down the coast to a restaurant that he assured her had a fine reputation. It was Italian, the sort of food she enjoyed, but she didn't feel hungry at all. She had hardly eaten all day and there was still this bewildered, brittle feeling inside her, a feeling she was fighting to control. She gladly allowed herself to be entertained and Shaw was certainly pouring on the charm. By the time he took her home, she felt as if she had known him for years.

Jim Sheldon rang the next afternoon with more entertainment.

'We're sailing this weekend,' he informed her in his bright, merry voice. 'Alice is dying to meet you. I've never stopped talking about that lunch. We wondered if you'd like to join us over Saturday and Sunday? It's not a big boat but we can carry three or four. As Ryan is away we wondered...?'

'I'd love to,' Lauren said quickly. It seemed that everyone knew that Ryan had deserted her; certainly Shaw knew. They probably knew too that Ryan was at his apartment with Janice Powers and they were feeling sorry for her as she was out at the beach house alone.

'Great! We'll pick you up Saturday early. Alice says shorts, swimsuit, deck shoes and one dress for a meal out. There's not much room for clothes on board.'

'Oh, dear,' Lauren laughed. 'Have I given the impression of being utterly devoted to fashion?'

'The impression you've made is stunning,' Jim said firmly. 'As to clothes, I'm only repeating my orders from Alice. She says that women like to know exactly what to wear. Er—bring your wooden spoon,' he added mischievously.

'I'm to be a seafaring cook?' Lauren asked in amusement and he sounded contrite.

'Just joking and dreaming. What a meal!'

Lauren was smiling as he rang off but she was also very thoughtful. She didn't want people taking her under their wing and she was sure they were feeling sorry for her. Still, she would go. A life had to be built that did not include Ryan and she had to make a start some time. This was as good as anything and it would get her away from here. She was missing him and her mind just wouldn't keep away from that apartment and his glamorous guest.

On Saturday morning, it was Shaw who called for her and he was looking very pleased with himself. Lauren soon found out why. He had managed to get himself invited along too. Lauren was glad. She knew him and found him pleasant company and although she had met Jim Sheldon several times and felt comfortable with him she had never even seen his wife Alice.

She need not have worried. Alice was watching for them, jumping about with enthusiasm as they parked on the quay. Like Jim, she was certainly not a slender shape, in fact she was decidedly plump, but she was sunny, smiling and attractive, her short dark curls bobbing about as she sprang down from the deck and hurled herself at Lauren.

'At last! I thought I was never going to get the chance to meet this wonder woman!'

'Hardly that,' Lauren laughed, submitting breathlessly to a long and vigorous handshake.

'According to Jim you're the world's best chef and according to Shaw the world's most beautiful woman. You notice he wheedled his way into this expedition?' she added in a whisper, glancing at the men who were talking boats in a very serious manner.

It was a smart, medium-sized launch and Lauren looked it over excitedly. She had never been on a boat like this before. Her only sailing had been across to

France on the ferry. She hoped she was not going to disgrace herself. The sea looked calm, though, and it was wonderfully hot. She should have been more than content but Ryan's face just wouldn't leave her mind. She wondered what he would have said if he had known about this trip.

'Why so gloomy? Not scared, are you?' Jim looked down at her from the deck, his cheeky grin cheering her up, and she smiled back, allowing herself to be helped on board by Shaw as Jim and Alice busily collected the few bits of luggage. In no time at all the powerful engines were throbbing and the launch moved smoothly away from its moorings and turned its nose to the open sea.

'Bliss!' Jim shouted. 'A whole weekend away from the trials and tribulations of the Landis Group. Even Ryan can't get at me now because he's flown out.'

'Already?' The words were out before Lauren could stop them and the others looked at her curiously.

'This morning. How did you come to miss it?' Jim turned back to his task but it was too late to slide out of things.

'Oh, he's been at the apartment,' Lauren managed blithely. 'We—we must have mixed up the date, I think. I imagined he was going on Monday for some reason or other.'

She didn't know if she had smoothed things over but she certainly had with Jim.

'Well, thank goodness it's today,' he laughed. 'He can't get me. I feel free! It wouldn't be the first time he's got me ship to shore and told me to come back.'

'Doesn't he allow free time?' Lauren was glad to keep the conversation away from her own slip and Jim shrugged good-naturedly.

'Why should he? He never has any free time himself. If he thinks of something he needs to check it with me very often.'

'And with me,' Shaw grumbled with a smile. 'Goodbye, Ryan. See you *much* later. Who's opening the drinks?'

Lauren lay back in the sunshine and tried to relax. Everything seemed to lead to Ryan. Even Jim's comment that Ryan had no time reminded her of what Ryan had said about never having the time to just sit and look at the sea. He never seemed to have been free of responsibility for the whole of his life and yet he had secretly made sure that she had as little responsibility as possible. Was that why? She just didn't understand. All she knew was that she couldn't seem to stop thinking about him.

'I wish he were here,' she suddenly burst out, and it brought forth howls of protest.

'Throw her over the side!' Jim roared. 'No mad-women allowed on this vessel!'

By the time the merriment had calmed she felt completely at home and determinedly shook off the miserable, lost feeling that had threatened to stay all day. Life went on without Ryan. She had things to plan but first she had to enjoy herself for two whole days. In any case, how did she know he had not taken Janice Powers with him to Canada? He might very well have done just that. Who would know? Not that Ryan had ever cared what people thought.

They were going to Monterey, the old Spanish capital of Upper California, and Lauren had nothing to do but sit back and enjoy the trip.

'Are you going to fish?' she asked Jim as she noticed the fishing tackle neatly stowed away.

'Not this time,' Alice cut in firmly. 'We're giving you a good time and letting you see a bit of the place. When

Ryan comes back I expect he'll have you locked away again.'

The comment surprised Lauren; it also made her flush slightly because she knew perfectly well that Ryan had now moved out for good.

'I don't know where you got that idea from,' she said with an uneasy laugh, turning to face Alice.

'I got it from Jim,' Alice confided, securely safe from her husband, who was talking loudly to Shaw. 'He mentioned that Ryan has a habit of appearing and either rescuing you or capturing you. He couldn't decide which it was. He also told me how the boss chopped Shaw smartly when he was being a little too admiring.' She suddenly giggled for all the world like a schoolgirl. 'Talk too much, don't I? Jim often threatens to gag me. I don't make a very good executive-type wife. No diplomacy.'

'You seem fine to me,' Lauren assured her earnestly. 'I don't think I could spend the day with one of those smart-suited, glamorous females who make big impressions.'

'Janice Powers,' Alice concluded with a sideways glance at her. 'Doesn't she just give you the shivers, though? At any function I sneak away as she approaches. Of course, between you and me, she's set on Ryan.'

'She did tell me that they went back a long way,' Lauren said uneasily. It really was asking for trouble to be discussing that woman when all she wanted to do was forget her altogether but there was an almost morbid desire to know how things really were between them.

Alice didn't know. If she had done, Lauren was sure she would have simply blurted it out.

'Oh, they go back a long way for sure. Just *how* they go back nobody knows. I happen to know that Ryan has taken her out more than once but with him you never can tell. It might very well have been business dinners.'

She suddenly laughed. 'Listen to me, telling you about Ryan. You're closer to him than anyone.'

'Not now,' Lauren confessed with a smile she felt was a bit tremulous. She suddenly didn't want to know another thing.

'Well,' Alice said comfortably, lying back and closing her eyes, 'I get most of my information from Jim and when I can stop myself from embroidering it for effect I'm pretty well informed about the old firm. Jim says that Ryan keeps a very special eye on you. He says that even when Ryan hasn't got a tight grip on your arm he's watching like a hawk.'

'That's to make sure I don't make a muddle of things,' Lauren said rather desperately, glad that dark glasses were hiding her eyes. 'I have a habit of stepping into trouble.'

'So have I!' Alice said gleefully. 'Isn't it fun? We should hit it off really well. Together we could upset a whole lot of people.'

Lauren started to laugh and felt herself relax. Any talk of Ryan tightened her up. She stayed with her eyes closed, soaking up the sun, listening to the hum of the engines, and she resolutely pushed him from her mind. She had no idea how she had managed to get into this state. Ryan had warned her that she was stepping into danger when she stepped close to him.

It was something she should not forget and it would be as well to keep in mind that he was not now the wonderful being who had guarded her through her early life. How would she feel if she met him now for the very first time? She turned on her side, almost groaning aloud. She would be fascinated and she knew it. Imagining him as a stranger was just about the most dangerous way of thinking about him.

CHAPTER EIGHT

MONTEREY at least took Lauren's mind off her immediate problems. She had thought that she might find herself left all day with Shaw—not that it bothered her but she needed the cheerful company of Alice more than anything else, and as they tied up at the marina Alice made it quite clear that she was not going to be pushed aside when she had found somebody after her own heart.

'There'll be a lot of girl talk,' she warned the men. 'Tag along but don't interrupt.'

Jim merely grinned benignly at his wife but Shaw looked a little downcast and Alice lowered her voice to whisper to Lauren.

'I think he was all set to keep you to himself but I'm really doing him a favour when you get right down to it. Ryan wouldn't be too happy to come back and find you entangled with Shaw.'

'I can see why you get into trouble and have to be gagged,' Lauren muttered, red-faced and wild-looking. 'Shaw seems quite respectable to me and, in any case, I'm not a child. Ryan and I live separate lives; we have done for years.'

'Just playing it safe,' Alice told her cheerfully, not even slightly put out at this. 'Anyway, we're eating first.'

Lauren hardly dared ask what they were doing second. They ate at one of the restaurants on Fisherman's Wharf. The food was good and they could watch the boats as they ate. Alice took up so much of the conversation that finally them two men gave up and talked to each other. If Shaw was annoyed, he certainly kept it to himself and

136

later as they walked round the old town, with its mixture of Spanish and American architecture, Lauren voiced a worry to Alice.

'Ryan wants me to have a team to help me,' she confessed. 'I'm not too keen but in a way he's right. If I should be ill or anything, his plans would go to pot and he wouldn't be too pleased. The trouble is, I don't even know how to begin looking for anyone.'

'Cooking, you mean?' Alice asked thoughtfully.

'That and everything else, although Maria and Constanza helped out the first time and it went well.'

'I might be able to hustle up two enthusiastic cooks,' Alice volunteered. 'There are a couple of girls close to us who are waiting to go to college. They probably couldn't be permanent but they'd put you on for a while until you get sorted out. Our son Bill dates Jane Price and she's mad about cooking, so is her friend Cynthia. Do you want me to give them a call?'

'Oh, if you would, Alice,' Lauren said eagerly. 'I—I was a bit stroppy with Ryan when he insisted...'

'And that's why he took off to the apartment?' Alice surmised, giving her a sidelong glance.

'No! Er—no, he just wanted to be close to work and I've got no other commitments until he comes back from Canada.' Lauren had to think fast to get herself out of the embarrassing situation but Alice merely looked thoughtful.

'Admitted, he spends a lot of time at the apartment,' she agreed unwillingly. 'It's close to work, couldn't be closer. Still, I had thought that with you there...'

'I'm a big girl,' Lauren said firmly. 'What about those two helpers?'

'I'll get to it the moment I get back home.' Alice let the subject of Ryan drop and Lauren was extremely grateful. She couldn't talk about him without getting a flushed face and queer feelings inside. It had to stop or she would never be able to face him again.

Jim proclaimed himself content to be a tourist but after a careful glance at Shaw Lauren doubted if he felt the same. Shaw was more at home doing smart things and by the time the lazy day was over and they had sailed back to their own moorings, halfway up the coast, his mouth looked a little tight. The evening was more to his liking—a nightclub—but even here he didn't get Lauren to himself; Alice was determinedly in every place.

'He'll thank me when Ryan gets back,' she said comfortably, and Jim nodded in agreement. Shaw was at the bar, looking none too pleased.

'More than likely he will,' Jim said firmly, backing his wife. 'Maybe Lauren won't, though?'

Lauren just laughed a trifle uneasily. She didn't know what to say. They had got it all wrong about Ryan. It was just his possessive, forceful manner. If they looked a little more carefully they would probably find he had that manner with most people he controlled. It was upsetting to admit that he controlled her when she had vowed not to let it happen. He was certainly controlling her mind, though. In spite of her weekend trip, her thoughts were still winging to Ryan whenever she relaxed for a moment.

During the following week, Alice arranged for the two students to visit Lauren and she took to them immediately. They were both enthusiastic and after a couple of days spent with her in the kitchen she knew they would be ideal. If they were not to be permanent then at least they would be a good start to her new attitude. She was about to be a boss whether she wanted to be or not.

It served to fill her days and Shaw seemed to be determined to fill her evenings. She got on very well with him and he was clearly proud of her appearance but every time he seemed to be about to get closer Lauren slid gracefully out of it. She didn't want a new boyfriend at all. She had almost forgotten Kent in such a short time and if she could do that, if she could make such a mistake as she had been doing, then she felt incapable of entering into any sort of close relationship. Besides, there was Ryan.

He rang from Canada during the week and Lauren's heart almost stopped at the sound of his voice. She had no idea what to say. They had neither seen each other nor spoken since that night in the rain and his voice reminded her so acutely that cold shivers raced over her skin before it flushed and heated. If she was about to be like this with one phone call, how would she be when she finally had to face him?

'Are you all right?' he asked quietly when, after saying hello, she said nothing else.

'Yes. I'm busy. I've been getting ready for the next meetings and I've been training two assistants. Alice found them for me—that's Alice Sheldon, you know. They're young but they know what they're doing and I like them. I think I might keep Maria and Constanza to serve, though, if you have no objection. I thought they did well and——' Having started, she couldn't seem to stop and Ryan interrupted firmly.

'Lauren! You can do whatever you want. Just calm down.'

'I—I am calm. What makes you say I'm not? How can you possibly know how I am when you're right up there...?'

She even heard the piteous sound of that herself and it silenced her completely. Ryan said nothing for a minute and she knew he would be feeling irritated. When he finally said her name she didn't answer.

'Lauren?' She just sat looking at the phone, feeling empty inside, and his tone softened a little. 'Are you still there or have you walked off? Try to make a signal. What about shouting down the phone?'

She found tears coming to her eyes and she blinked them away rapidly. You could tell a lot over the phone, whatever people thought, and she wasn't going to have Ryan thinking she was crying about him. She had never done that in her life.

'I'm sorry I went off and left you,' he said quietly. 'I had no right to treat you like that.'

'I'm perfectly happy. I've been enjoying myself.'

'Have you?' His voice was such a dark murmur that the threatening tears began to fall down her cheeks. 'Jim tells me he's done his best. How did you like the boat?'

'You've been checking up?' She just gulped the words, terribly guilty that she had not told him herself immediately but he didn't seem to be annoyed.

'Didn't you expect it? I left you there alone.'

'You mean they came to my rescue because of you and not because they—they like me?'

'I mean nothing of the sort!' By now he *did* seem annoyed. 'Is it going to be impossible to make any comment without you thinking the worst of me? I had to be in touch with Jim and he passed on the information.'

Of course, he would have, she could see that, and now she was contrite.

'I—I'm sorry. Maybe I'm a little edgy.'

'Maybe we both are,' Ryan growled irritably. 'It's hardly surprising.' He suddenly sighed and evidently got control of his rising anger. 'Look, I'll be back soon. Make your mind up that we're going to talk, because we most certainly are.'

'About what?' It was suddenly tricky again, dangerous, but, more than that, she didn't want Ryan to say anything that would drive her away from him. Missing him for this little time had made her realise how much she would miss him if she never saw him again.

'You know what we have to talk about,' he told her sharply and the panic simply grew. He was going to say this wouldn't work out. Perhaps he was going to send her back to England.

'I can manage anything,' she said in an agitated voice. 'I'm not bothered about you going away. I don't want us to change, Ryan.'

'We have changed, Lauren,' he reminded her quietly. 'There's no going back and you understand that perfectly well. Sometimes it's just not possible to ignore things. Some things just don't go away, however much you want them to.'

He sounded terribly weary and he just rang off with no further words, leaving her shattered. It had all seemed final. He was about to send her away because he wanted her and couldn't accept it. She lay back and closed her eyes. Neither could she. She had seen him as a stranger, looked at him with different eyes, cast off her childhood hero and found another person in Ryan.

Now he was not her dearest Ryan, her friend and helper. Now he excited her and left her looking at others with critical eyes. One love had turned to another and she had no idea what to do.

It was this odd desperation that drove her to action. She sat glumly weighing things up and even went to have a good look at herself in the mirror in her room. What on earth was happening to her? She was almost creeping about for fear of offending Ryan. If he felt incapable of being here with her, what was she about to do—sit down and shrivel? She decided to give a party.

So far she knew hardly anyone and if she was to stay in California that would have to change. Ryan had said she could do anything she wanted, so why not? She rang Alice and her idea was greeted with all the glee she could have hoped for.

'Great! It's a super idea, just a little like having a secret party while the parents are away, the sort of things we used to do as kids.'

'I hope you don't mean Ryan,' Lauren ventured cautiously. 'He's hardly a parent figure.'

'But Lauren, he's the big boss! The idea of having a party at his place while he's in Canada is a scream.'

'He knows all about it and approves,' Lauren lied quickly, thinking very little of her plan now. 'I live here too, don't forget. You make it sound as if we're about to break into somebody's house and wreck it. I want to meet people. Ryan wants me to meet people. I'm supposed to be building a new life here. Anyway, I want to try out a few recipes and I want to give the girls some practice.'

'Just joking,' Alice laughed. 'Don't sound so English. Looking forward to your food. I'll make a list of possible guests.'

'It's semi-formal,' Lauren got in hastily, her mind on some wild party that would spread to the beach, the last thing she wanted. It wasn't going to be that sort of food.

'Sure,' Alice agreed comfortably.

By the time she put the phone down, Lauren wasn't too sure about her brilliant idea. Alice sounded more like a middle-aged delinquent every day. The die was cast, though, and she really did need to see how her new assistants coped under pressure. She rang them up and they were ecstatic, anything for a party apparently. Lauren sighed and felt even more unsure of her idea. She had quite forgotten that this was California. She hoped that Alice wouldn't see Ryan for some time. She might just start telling him how much he approved of this plan and it was very easy to imagine Ryan's caustic comments.

As things worked out, it could not have been better. The girls managed beautifully and Maria and Constanza were delighted with this turn of events.

'Not many parties here, Señorita Lauren,' Maria confided in the middle of everything, with the music going and people enjoying the food. 'Now you here we have happy times every week.'

Lauren didn't think so. She wasn't at all sure what Ryan would think of this particular happy time. She wasn't too happy herself anyhow although she smiled until her face felt stiff. At least she was meeting people and her mind was now quite secure on the subject of the suitability of Jane and Cynthia.

'You look lovely—a dream,' Shaw murmured, coming up to her as she stood by herself for a minute, watching the guests. 'A dream who can cook. What more would anyone want?'

Lauren was pleased to see that he was grinning. Coping with this was easy, coping with an amorous venture was quite beyond her nowadays. Her cool sophistication seemed to have gone. All she felt now was vulnerable, increasingly so.

'You're very gallant,' she joked. She knew she looked good tonight; it was and always had been her way of disguising anxiety. Clothes were something she was never short of and now she was wearing a very expensive dress, a sheath of dark blue silk with an overlay of patterned chiffon slit up the sides. Her fair hair hung gleaming to her shoulders, framing a slightly flushed face.

'I'm always gallant,' Shaw complained. 'If you wore shoes instead of those,' he added, glancing at her dainty silver sandals with high heels, 'I'd probably drink champagne out of one of them.'

'A revolting thought,' Lauren laughed but he suddenly moved closer.

'Romantic,' he corrected quickly. 'I could get very romantic about you, Lauren.'

'Please don't.' She still tried to joke but the party suddenly seemed just a little remote, no help at all. They were standing by the door into the hall, well back from the others; even the noise and music was no assistance.

'It's too late,' Shaw laughed, wrapping his arms around her. 'I've been wanting to kiss you since I first saw you. It's all the party I need. I can manage without the music.'

'Shaw!' Lauren belatedly tried to draw back but he only laughed.

'I love that stiff, English attitude, honey. It's such an excitement.' He pulled her close and Lauren gathered all her lost sophistication around her, holding him off and smiling coolly, making it a joke because she didn't quite know what else to do. She didn't know exactly what to say either. It was all unexpected. If Shaw had wanted to try something like this he had had plenty of opportunity when he had taken her out before.

'Shaw!' She said his name quite sharply but she never had to say anything else at all because at that moment Ryan walked in.

He came through from the veranda, his bag in his hand, and his eyes went straight to her, their vivid green hardening to crystal brilliance as they summed up the situation.

'Oh, my God!' Shaw muttered, his arms falling away from Lauren instantly. Ryan tossed his bag down on a chair and strolled across to them with deceptive indolence.

'Drunk?' he enquired silkily, his eyes pinning Shaw.

'Probably.' Shaw's face reddened and he suddenly looked just a little like a guilty boy. Lauren felt guilty too although she couldn't think of a thing she had done to justify the feeling.

'Take a walk on the beach,' Ryan advised softly, his gaze never leaving Shaw. 'It will either kill or cure. The sea air brings you to your senses or makes you keel over. I await the outcome with interest.'

It was not in any way a suggestion and Shaw simply obeyed, disappearing through the huge glass doors as if he were programmed to proceed. That was when the green eyes moved to Lauren and they were no less hard.

'Are we having fun?' Ryan asked harshly, and Lauren's ready temper began to boil. What was she scared of, for heaven's sake? He was treating her like a child again.

'Well, we were,' she countered defiantly. 'As you can see, a party is in progress. Are you going to order them all out?'

'Now what gave you that idea?' He smiled at her menacingly. 'I can see a few of my friends here. I intend to change and join in merrily.'

'You made Shaw look a fool!' Lauren snapped and his sardonic smile deepened.

'He needed assistance? Fools are not made, they're born.'

'Ryan! You're back!' Alice sailed up, flushed and smiling, not one bit put out. 'You caught us at it; I was sort of hoping you would. It's wonderfully wicked to have a party at a person's house when they're away. Lauren said you knew and approved, though, so that took a bit of the shine off it.' She kissed Ryan's cheek, laughing up at him, and he shot a glance at Lauren that was a bit like the worst kind of lightning.

'Of course I approve,' he said with a much more pleasant smile as it was for Alice. 'I'm sorry you feel it would have been better to sneak about it. You must have been a very difficult teenager.'

'Was Lauren?' Alice countered pertly, looking from one to the other with bright-eyed interest.

'Not that I noticed,' Ryan murmured. 'Keep on with the party, Alice. I'll get changed and join you. Jim here?' he added, glancing round.

'You betcha,' Alice chortled. 'Catch Jim missing a party. I'll tell him you're here. I saw you come in but everyone else was too busy enjoying themselves to notice you.'

'So I observed,' Ryan said quietly, making Lauren's cheeks flush again. 'I'll see you later.' He turned to Lauren as Alice walked away. 'What a pity I didn't know about my own approval. I could have brought my own partner.' His sardonic glance slid round the room. 'Very chic,' he murmured. 'Very London. Just the sort of thing Janice would like. Next time you give a party please invite her.' He walked back to collect his bag and Lauren found her feet wouldn't move. She had been severely chastised and she felt too hurt to really retaliate.

His glance raked over her as he came back towards the hall.

'I hope you saved me some of your fabulous food, enchanting lady. As I knew about the party I assume you knew I would want feeding. Without food, my approval might thin out rapidly.'

He walked out and Lauren stormed after him into the faint privacy of the hall.

'You told me I could do as I liked!' she reminded him heatedly, hurt swallowed and pride surfacing. 'You also told me that I live here. That being the case, I can't see anything wrong with a party.'

An imperious hand tilted her face and Ryan looked down at her coolly.

'Nothing is wrong with the party,' he conceded quietly. 'Did I give that impression?' He was watching her arrogantly, a tyrant, and Lauren's eyes snapped sparks.

'You gave the impression of throwing Shaw out!'

'Oh? We're discussing Shaw, are we?' he enquired infuriatingly. 'I thought we were speaking about the party. I'll gladly change the subject if you wish but you know how it is with approval—now you have it, now you don't.'

He walked off and left her standing there, glaring after him, and after one frustrating minute she went back into the other room. It was her party and she would now have to find Shaw and make him feel better when she would rather have slapped his face. She did take a quick precaution first. She darted into the kitchen and told Maria that Ryan was back and would want food. It was a relief to see that there was some left although Maria's face fell a little and clearly she and Constanza had had their eyes on it for themselves. They would have to do without. The tyrant with green eyes needed soothing. After all, she had to face him later.

By the time Lauren had finished her anxious little chores, Shaw was back. He had joined the others and was looking very grim indeed as she went to him.

'I'm really sorry about that,' Lauren said quietly, but he smiled ruefully and shook his head.

'No, *I* am. It was my fault—playing with fire. An odd characteristic for a lawyer, don't you think? I knew better even while I was doing it. Not that I expected him to walk in when he did. I imagined he was still safely in Canada.'

'So did I,' Lauren confessed and he glanced at her wryly.

'Not that it would have made much difference. You were clearly not about to offer me more than a sharp slap. As it was, you didn't need to make the effort. The tiger was back, guarding his cub.' He looked at her intently. 'Or is it his mate?'

'I can do without that kind of remark!' Lauren said sharply, her face flushing instantly.

'No insult intended. Not that any of this is my business, and if I've any sense, which I have, I'll not try to make it my business. It's pretty obvious, though, that something deep and vibrant runs between you and our powerful boss.'

'He's my stepbrother,' Lauren said desperately, but he shook his head and reached out for a drink as Maria sailed past with a tray.

'He's a lot more than that, beautiful, even if you don't know it.' He glanced up and then looked quickly at her again. 'He's appeared and I'm about to guard my back. Forgive me, honey, but I value both my neck and my job.'

He made a very good show of drifting away nonchalantly and Ryan's voice came almost in her ear a second later.

'Discretion, a valuable asset to an ambitious and rising company lawyer,' he murmured sardonically. 'I can see that his head has cleared.'

'Ryan! Why are you——?'

Lauren turned to him in agitation but he turned her away again, his arm coming round her waist instantly.

'Hush,' he said darkly. 'A united front as always. Introduce me to our guests and then feed me. Later—we talk.'

'I don't want to talk,' Lauren muttered but he tightened his hold on her slender waist, hurting her just a little, leading her on whether she wanted to go or not.

'No scenes, no fuss,' he advised threateningly. 'Remember who you are.'

'I don't damned well know!' Lauren snapped in a little voice and his arm drew her closer until she was tucked under under his shoulder.

'Then it's about time you found out. For now, though, you have guests, and as I live here too and most certainly approve, having been told so clearly by Alice, we face them together.'

He was instantly the very life of the party and at first Lauren thought he was not about to let her go even one step away. He did, though. Apparently it was just his way of showing everyone that she was his protégée. Her eye caught Shaw's as Ryan finally let her go and joined Jim and Alice, and Shaw raised his glass, giving her a rather sardonic salute.

Several other eyes were on her and Lauren had to fight hard to maintain a carefree expression. It was obvious what they thought. It was even obvious what Alice and Jim thought. As to herself, she didn't know anything. Ryan was fencing her in and she had no idea if it was because he was jealous or if it was because he had determined to guide her steps as usual.

One thing she did know—she was not about to face any 'talk' this evening because she didn't feel able to cope with it. He was either going to say that this was not working out according to his plans and she would have to go back to England, or he was going to make some permanent living arrangement for her that would keep her out of his hair.

As to wanting her, if he still did, that was not a thing that would bother Ryan overmuch. He had a will of iron. He also had Janice Powers. If that woman was going to be invited here then Lauren wanted to go anyway. Unexpectedly, jealousy bit into her like a pain. She had felt it before with Ryan but not since she was eighteen. Now it raged through her, almost making her bend over in agony.

Her eyes searched for him but he was not looking at her at all. He was laughing and talking to some sun-bronzed and beautiful woman who looked as if she had never felt any sort of indecision in her life. Ryan was like that too. Lauren's eyes lingered on him, unable to leave him. Tall and lean, handsome and completely in control, he was now wearing casual clothes that breathed expense. He was with his own sort of people. He had lived a life for years that she knew nothing of at all. The feeling of being a burden was overwhelming and her expression was unknowingly indicative of everything she felt.

Ryan glanced up and caught her looking at him and, like Shaw, he raised his glass but the same old smile tilted his lips, mockingly amused, wryly entertained, as if she were a well-known half-wit. Lauren turned impatiently away and threw herself heart and soul into the party. If she wore herself out she might sleep.

After a few minutes, the dark voice was in her ear again and Ryan's hand came to her arm.

'Feed me,' he ordered, his hand sliding down her arm to her wrist, but she was ready for him and she turned to him with a glittering smile.

'Of course.' She looked towards the door and raised her hand and the ever-ready Maria grinned and reappeared with food, making her way towards them skilfully.

'Very professional,' Ryan murmured. 'I thought you would have to venture into the kitchen all by yourself.'

'I'm entertaining my guests,' Lauren reminded him pertly. 'It's all part of the training.'

'And very impressive until the mask slips,' Ryan said softly. He left her and found himself a place to eat and Lauren tried very hard not to look at him again. He was very subtly different—worrying. She might be able to keep her head turned away but she was aware of him to such an extent that waves of an invisible current seemed to join them.

Nobody seemed to wish to leave and it even looked as if Ryan was encouraging them to stay. The strain mounted as far as Lauren was concerned so that when they began to drift away in small, laughing groups she was almost ready to scream.

Ryan caught her wrist as she passed him and once again pulled her to his side.

'Surely we're going to wave them from the premises and send them happily on their way?'

'I'm just going to see that the kitchen is cleared and—and everything is in order,' Lauren managed quickly. 'I have to thank everyone.'

'What about paying your staff?' He was suddenly serious, the sharp edge of derision dropping away as if it had never been there at all.

'That's a problem. I'll pay Jane and Cynthia when the next business lunch takes place.'

She refused to admit that her own resources were now very limited and Ryan gave her a keen glance.

'I would think that a couple of pre-college girls would be fairly hard up. Arrange to send them a cheque. I intended to set you up with banking facilities but it slipped my mind.'

'I won't be kept!' Lauren looked at him angrily and he tilted her chin, the mockery back with a vengeance.

'Kept from what? You're on the payroll and that includes expenses. As far as I can see, your small but efficient staff are very much expenses, so arrange to send them a cheque. We'll fix it up tomorrow.'

'Are you staying?' She didn't know if she was delighted or scared.

'I haven't decided.' He turned away to wave goodbye to a group of people. 'For now, let's just say that I'm back.'

Suddenly his attitude was dismissive and as a couple of people came up to talk to him Lauren escaped and went to deal with her staff. He was quite right. She was now a working girl, working for the Landis Group. She straightened her slender shoulders and marched off. It was time she took an attitude herself and the cool, efficient business lady was as good a one as any.

Her expression set into her new role, she came back to see the last of the guests off and took her place by Ryan with a very glittering smile on her face.

'You're sure lucky to be living here in this wonderful house,' one bronzed and languid young lady said, her admiring glance on Ryan's coolly handsome face. Lauren saw the corner of his mouth quirk and she knew he had heard.

'Yes, it's certainly nice to have a wealthy guardian,' she said sweetly. 'It gives one such a feeling of security.'

It gained her more than one odd look but she didn't care. As far as she was concerned there was nobody in the world but Ryan and herself and she intended to hold her own with cool sophistication.

CHAPTER NINE

IT DESERTED Lauren as the last car pulled away and Maria popped her head round the hall door to bid them goodnight. It was suddenly very quiet and more than a little tense.

'Let's talk,' Ryan said calmly, but Lauren's calm went flying away on very swift wings.

'I don't want to.' She moved away but Ryan turned to face her with an expression that told her he was not at all interested in her wishes.

'It's a necessity, otherwise I wouldn't bother tonight.' Without appearing to have moved he had cut off her retreat to her own room and Lauren felt at bay. Not only was he standing there, tall and magnificent, he was pinning her with those eyes, and they were a little too clearly green for her liking. It spelled trouble.

'There's tomorrow,' she said firmly.

'It *is* tomorrow.' He glanced at his watch. 'It's two in the morning and I have a meeting before lunch. I am then booked on the New York flight and I won't be back until the weekend, maybe later.'

Dismay flooded through Lauren, quietening her agitation. He was leaving again and he wanted things settled before he came back. He probably wanted her miles away before then too.

'Do you always go away like this?' she asked miserably, meeting his eyes now and not trying to duck out.

'Usually.' He shrugged and gave a slight smile. 'Nothing takes care of itself. Let's not get side tracked. I want to talk to you.'

'When you come back.' She turned to the veranda and escape. There was something so determined about Ryan tonight that she knew for sure she was not going to like what he had to say. She didn't want to know because whatever it was it would make her unhappy.

'Lauren!' His patience finally snapped and he spoke sharply. It was enough to send her swiftly out on to the veranda and as he moved too she ran down the steps and on to the beach, pulling off her sandals and running through the soft sand away from the house.

She was quite well aware that this was a display of lunacy that would infuriate him but she couldn't stay and have a serious discussion about any sort of arrangement he had planned for her. She didn't want him to plan things for her. She just wanted to be with him and it was obvious that he didn't want that. There had been no sign of softness about him tonight, no evidence that he had been as desperate to see her as she had been to see him.

The wind was blowing the chiffon of her dress out behind her like butterfly wings and as she slowed, breathless and feeling foolish, Ryan grasped her arm and spun her round. She hadn't even been aware that he was following and she began to struggle at once.

'I don't want to talk!' She tried to get away but it was quite impossible and Ryan's eyes glittered with anger.

'As your *guardian* I feel quite within my rights to insist,' he bit out and Lauren's face flushed even more.

'I only said that because . . .'

'Because there's a lot of speculation about us? I know,' he agreed harshly. 'It had not escaped my attention.'

That quite convinced her what this talk was to be about and she stopped struggling, feeling weary and quite bereft.

'I—I suppose you feel it's necessary to do something about it?' she whispered. 'I understand the position you're in.'

'The position I'm in? Idle speculation doesn't much bother me.' His hands tightened on her bare arms. 'I haven't seen you for quite a few days until tonight. The last time I saw you is what lingers in my mind.'

'It was a fit of madness,' Lauren said quickly, not able to look higher than his chest. Without her shoes she felt particularly defenceless and her eyes were drawn to the brown column of his throat where the expensive soft shirt lay open. 'I'm well aware that it was just a fit of madness. I'll just forget it.'

'You're very understanding,' Ryan murmured scathingly. 'However, much as I appreciate your kindness, I don't feel able to forget it myself. Therefore, we talk.'

'No!' Lauren pulled herself free and turned but she never even managed one step. He pounced on her and she was swept off her feet, not to be held in his arms but to be thrown over his shoulder like a bundle of feathers, and he turned back to the house, striding out angrily and utterly ignoring her protests.

She felt ungainly, belittled and tearful. More than that, the blood was rushing to her head, making her feel dizzy, and she clutched at his belt to steady herself because he was making no allowances for her predicament; his stride was not at all careful and she was bouncing about with no way of helping herself.

'Ryan! Put me down!' It was even painful to speak, hanging upside-down, a new discovery that she could have done without. He never bothered to answer and she tried to hold her head still but it didn't help at all.

'Please, Ryan! I'm dizzy!'

He put her on to her feet and she could see that they were at the veranda steps. She couldn't see them very well, though, because everything was spinning and she had a nasty feeling that she was going to be sick.

'Oh!' She swayed, her hand coming to her head, and Ryan caught her before she could fall. He pulled her towards him, folding her into his arms, and she rested her forehead against his chest as the nausea faded and the stars stopped spinning before her eyes. 'I'm all right,' she managed faintly and Ryan drew back to look at her with derisive amusement.

'You must be more delicate than I remember. When I toss Janice over my shoulder, she never turns a hair.'

'That's probably because it's all lacquered to her head!' Lauren snapped, finding the will to glare up at him, and he was laughing down at her, thoroughly enjoying her discomfort.

'Why, sugar, you're jealous,' he accused softly, and Lauren went wildly into action, her fists clenched and beating at his chest, hot tears beginning to pour down her face at this easy cruelty. Of course, he was enjoying all this. She was ridiculous. She had made a fool of herself again as she always did with Ryan and she could just imagine him walking along with Janice over his shoulder, both of them laughing. It was running before her mind like a film.

'I hate you, Ryan! I really hate you!' she sobbed, pummelling his chest with both fists together.

'If I thought you really did,' he said harshly, 'I'd let you go.'

'You're letting me go! You're going to *make* me go!' Lauren cried bitterly. Tears were glittering on her face. The moon on one side, riding high above the sea, and the house lights on the other made her misery very plain to observe and Ryan pulled her back to him, his thumbs wiping at her tears before he drew her head to his shoulder and rocked her in strong arms.

'When have I ever let you go?' he asked wearily. 'I've never been able to manage it.'

She looked up then and he was watching her face with gleaming eyes, the tilted enigmatic smile on his lips, and she shook her head slowly, unable to follow his thoughts this time.

'But that was what the talk was going to be about—wasn't it?' she whispered. He never answered. He just looked at her, his eyes searching her upturned face and then his arms tightened and he caught her closer, his mouth capturing hers.

It was the ghost from the past she had wanted to grasp. It was the piece of jigsaw fitting into place. The heat ran through her as it had done before and Lauren just melted into him, her lips soft and clinging beneath his. Her slender arms wound around his neck and when he drew her down to the veranda steps she lay against him, eagerly accepting the kisses he placed on her face and neck, her mouth turned up to his when he came back to claim it.

There was a tremendous urgency about him that sent her emotions reeling and she was not aware of anything but the desire to be everything he wanted. His hands moved over her, caressing her through the thin material of her dress. His mouth was hard and warm, parting her lips, devouring her in an overwhelming invasion of passion.

'Lauren!' He groaned her name and pulled her tightly against him, his lips still planting heated kisses on her neck and face. 'This is what we have to talk about,' he said fiercely. 'I want you! I want you badly. Stay with me and I'm not going to be able to stop. Every time I reach for you you'll offer me what I want and I'm not even sure if you know what you're doing.'

'I do! I do know what I'm doing!' Lauren protested shakily but his hands cupped her face and he stared down at her in the lights with glittering eyes.

'Do you? Did you know what you were doing when you almost got engaged to Redmond? You were going to marry him!' His voice almost choked on the last two words and Lauren's hand came out to touch his face.

'It's different, Ryan. It's different with you.'

'Is it?' He let her go and turned away, shrugging her hand from his face with an impatience that showed his surging feelings. 'And what about Shaw Newark? Where does he fit into your emotions?'

Lauren drew back with a little sob, turning her face away.

'That's not fair! You know I don't want Shaw close like—like that.'

'Like what?' he bit out harshly, turning on her. 'You like his attention but you don't want to be in his bed? You'd better sort out your feelings before you decide to stay here, then, because I want you in *my* bed!'

She closed her eyes and then opened them quickly, looking down at her own clenched hands.

'Is that all it is? Is that my choice? Stay here and sleep with you or go back to London and safety? I'll *go!*'

She jumped up and fled across the veranda, running up to her room. He didn't love her. All that was saving her was the past, the wonderful past when he had been her giant, her prince, her lingering dream. She was just another girl, somebody he wanted.

In her room she stood with her head bowed, feeling as if every bone in her body was aching with longing. She was too hurt for tears and she only just realised that she still had her sandals. All this time the thin silver straps had been looped around her wrist. She dropped them to the floor, wanting to sink down with them.

A noise made her turn her head and Ryan was standing there, looking at her starkly, his gaze moving over her white face, over the tousled beauty of her shining hair.

'I don't want you to go,' he said quietly. 'I'm not even sure I could let you go if you begged.' His face was pale too, looking as strained as her own.

'You—you don't have any faith in me,' she whispered, hanging her head. 'You don't even believe that I know my own mind.'

'A little while ago you were getting married,' he said in a tight voice. He suddenly ran his fingers through his hair frustratedly. 'My God! What's happening to me? I want you whether you know your own mind or not!'

'You weren't there.' Lauren looked up and spoke very quietly. 'It's true, I didn't know my own mind. I was always looking for something—waiting.'

'What were you waiting for?' Ryan was watching her intently, a muscle leaping at the side of his mouth, tension on his face. 'What were you looking for?'

'The past. My ghosts, my dreams. I didn't really know.'

'But you know now?' he asked tautly and she looked back into his eyes with certainty as she nodded.

'Yes, I know.'

'And what do you know, Lauren?'

'You came back into my life. You're here. I don't know anything else. I'm not even sure of anything else except that—that...' Her teeth tugged at her lower lip. Tears welled into her eyes and Ryan's face softened.

'Do you want your door open or closed?' he asked quietly.

'Closed.' Lauren blinked at the tears. He was going. Once again his iron control had won.

'Ask me to stay on this side when I close it,' he said huskily and her head shot up, sparks tingling all over her. She couldn't even speak, her parted lips wouldn't

seem to work but those strange green eyes turned dark
and his hand reached out behind him to close the door,
his gaze never leaving her face. The door clicked shut
as she ran towards him and his arms were reaching for
her even before she got there.

'*Lauren*!' he groaned. 'I can't sleep without you for
another night of my life.'

'You don't have to,' she said tremulously. She stood
on tiptoe so that her lips could reach his face. 'Whatever
you want me to be...'

'Sometimes I could beat you!' His mouth came down
on her urgently and then lifted again, leaving her, and
she gave a small whimpering cry, her hands circling his
neck, trying to bring him back to her.

'Ryan!' She saw the old quirk to his lips and her face
looked mournful. 'You're being cruel to me,' she whispered accusingly and sparks seemed to fly from his
fingertips as his hands shaped her body almost roughly.

'Maybe I should be.' He looked down at her and his
eyes seemed to be on fire. 'Right now, though, I just
don't have the time.'

'I want to stay with you always, always,' she whispered distractedly and he pulled her tightly against him,
her name a soft murmur on his lips. She was soft and
desirable and he moulded her to his taut body, his hands
sliding round her hips to bring her even closer. She felt
his surging arousal and her body lay softly against him,
a trembling sigh escaping from her lips as he slid the zip
of her dress down and let the cool night air fan her skin.

'Tonight I want to kiss you all over,' he murmured
thickly. He slid the dress from her shoulders, leisurely
guiding it over her arms, his warm breath fanning her
shoulder. He trailed his lips over her skin, making her
shiver in anticipation, and then his hands made a slow,
possessive journey from her waist to the swollen beauty
of her breasts.

'Ryan!' Her arms encircled his neck as his palms caressed the hard, sharp peaks and for a second he looked into her eyes. His face was taut, almost harsh, his eyes glazed, his irregular breathing mingling with her own gasping breaths. 'Ryan!' She tossed her head back wantonly and his head bent as he nipped painfully at the skin of her neck.

'A brand,' he said thickly, '*my* brand!'

When she opened her eyes and looked at him, his eyes were smouldering, darker than they had ever been, and he twisted her against him, pushing the zip all the way, letting the dress slide to the floor, and then he curled her up into his arms, lifting her and walking to the bed.

Her own arms were so tightly round his neck that he had to forcibly release them and she tried to twist away from him as he gazed down at her body where only the tiniest of lacy briefs hid her from his gaze. He turned her back possessively, his mouth sensual as his eyes ran over her with heated satisfaction.

'This is not new,' he said huskily. 'I've imagined it a thousand times, over and over like a drug.' He pulled his shirt over his head and let it drop to the floor, his eyes still on her. 'You're scared,' he said softly and her face flushed like a rose.

'Only because—because . . .'

'I know. If this had happened to you before I think I'd go mad. I want to kill anyone who looks at you.' He came down to her, gathering her close, his hand gently sliding away her last flimsy garment. 'I won't frighten you, darling,' he murmured against her lips. 'All I want to do is make you mine at last, really mine, not some dream in your head, not some imagined hero. I'm real, Laurie, hurting, aching. Are you aching for me?'

'Yes, oh, yes!' She pressed herself closer, her fingertips tracing his face, and his hand fastened in her hair as he pulled her head back and began to kiss her, hard possessive kisses that drove out any last shreds of fear. His body was warm against hers, warm and powerful, strange after all the years of knowing him. He trailed kisses to her breasts and over the tense arc of her stomach. His lips were like fire on her skin as his kisses circled her waist and Lauren clutched him closer, moaning softly, her hands tugging at his belt until he drew back and slid the rest of his clothes away.

'Is this what you want, sweetheart?' His body came over hers completely, forcing her into the soft coolness of the bed, and her legs parted to allow her to get even closer. She could feel his skin against hers, his warmth, his power, the hard masculine body held back even if only by a fraction of space. She moved against him eagerly and he gave a shuddering sigh, his head bending as he took one rosy nipple in his teeth and tugged gently.

Lauren gave a sharp, gasping cry, her body quivering with tension when he drew the pained nipple into his mouth and soothed it. She began to twist wildly beneath him as his hand covered the throbbing warmth and his lips moved to the other breast.

She was in some golden, heated dream but it was real. She was here with Ryan! Her hands searched his skin, her fingers sliding over the curve of his spine, her palms sliding down over his lean hips to caress him as he was caressing her.

'Don't.' His voice was softly shaken as his lips tasted the corners of her mouth. 'Keep on doing that and I'll forget how new this is to you.'

'Forget! Please forget!' she begged and his mouth crushed hers forcefully as his control snapped and he claimed the moist sweetness at the heart of her being.

'Laurie!' He felt the warmth envelop him and he was beyond any stopping. 'I've waited so long for this.' He moved more deeply inside her and Lauren gasped with pain and then relaxed into the bliss of being part of Ryan.

Her hands clutched at him and then wound around his neck as warmth flooded through her and the ache inside grew to a crescendo of longing.

He lifted her closer, the driving power of his body making her weak with pleasure and his lips searched blindly to fuse with hers as she slid off the earth into warm, velvet darkness that promised the light of the sun.

'Ryan! Ryan!' She came back to earth calling his name and he was hovering over her, still part of her. His eyes were brilliant, vibrant, thrillingly possessive, and that old smile twisted his lips.

'Welcome back,' he said softly, his hand coming to stroke her face gently as she gazed at him in wonder. 'You nearly got away there.'

'I—I didn't know that . . .'

His eyes darkened and his smile grew, his mouth sensuous.

'What do you know now?'

'I don't want you to leave me,' she whispered, and his mouth covered her trembling lips for a long time until flames started to ignite inside her again and Ryan's body hardened against hers. He tore his lips away and looked at her ruefully.

'You have this odd effect on me,' he confessed huskily. 'You make me greedy.'

'Me too.' She felt safe, warm, as luxurious as a cat, and she stretched sinuously, her slender leg moving against his, and Ryan's face tightened.

'Laurie,' he muttered. 'You little witch.'

She was smiling like a siren, her eyes beckoning, and when she wound herself around him he pulled her close almost roughly, letting her feel the power she was wilfully unleashing.

'Tomorrow, you'll regret this wild behaviour,' he threatened, his hands arching her closer with almost painful possessiveness.

'It's tonight,' she whispered, and with a low growl he came back to her, claiming her with a demanding urgency that took her breath away.

'Tell me you want to be part of me for every minute of your life,' he commanded harshly.

'You know I do.'

'Say it!' His hand fastened in her hair, forcing her head up, and she looked at him in bewilderment, not understanding the emotions that raced across his face—passion, pain and something else she could not even guess at. She couldn't answer and her silent bewilderment melted his fierce looks. He brought her tightly to him, his passion tempered to her more tender body.

'Oh, Laurie,' he breathed against her lips. 'Laurie, my impossible darling.'

Next morning, Ryan wasn't there when Lauren woke up. For a minute she closed her eyes again and tried to think clearly. The pieces of her life seemed to have slotted into place with no warning. All the waiting, all the restless searching had only been because of Ryan. Even though she had not known how much she loved him, her heart had known all by itself. She had been waiting for Ryan all her life. There had never been anyone else at all.

In the long hours before dawn he had never spoken of love. He had called her darling, made love to her with passion and tenderness, but he had not spoken one word to set her mind at rest. There had been a sort of desperation about him that she had not been able to soothe and it left a worrying doubt at the back of her mind. What would they do now? He had never said.

She was resting back, thinking about everything, when Ryan came into the room and stood looking at her. He was dressed ready to leave, his jacket slung over his shoulder.

'I'm going,' he said quietly, his eyes intently on her. She flushed with shyness, well aware that only the sheet covered her from his sight. His announcement threw her into a panic too.

'Going? Where? Surely it's not time?' She sat up, keeping the sheet twisted round her, her shyness pushed aside at the thought of being without him.

'It's almost ten,' he pointed out. 'I have a meeting at eleven-thirty. I can't stay any longer.'

'When will you get back from New York?' It was impossible to keep the disappointment out of her voice and he walked across to her, tossing his jacket to a chair, sitting on the bed beside her.

'The weekend probably. I'm not sure. It depends how it goes. There'll be a small board meeting while I'm away,' he added, looking at her consideringly. 'Jim will chair it for me. They'll want feeding. Think you can manage it?'

'Of course.' She drew her knees up and rested her chin on them, not looking at him because she wanted to beg him to stay. 'I'm working for you, after all. It will give me the chance to let the new staff show their mettle. How many?'

'Contact Jill. She'll have the details.' He suddenly ran his hand over her hair. 'You're very businesslike this morning. Do you only soften at night?'

It added to her feeling of shyness, to her helpless longing to be close to him, and she never answered.

'Laurie?' His voice was softly enquiring and when she looked up his face was softened too, his eyes darkening more every second. He looped her fair hair back behind her ears, his glance moving across her face, searching every inch of it. 'You haven't changed much since eighteen,' he murmured. 'Still the same astonishing fairness, still the same dark eyes that promise so many things.' He ran his hand down her bare arm, making her tingle. 'Still the same slender arms that wind around my neck.' He tilted her face back as his mouth twisted sensually. 'Don't expect me to regret last night. It's what I wanted when I took you to your first dinner-dance.'

Her eyes opened wide and he smiled into them.

'You didn't know that, did you, my tempting little witch? You complained that nobody noticed you. God! I noticed you. I wanted you enough to take you then.'

Lauren gave a small gasping cry and he pulled her forward into his arms, pushing the concealing sheet aside, capturing her mouth urgently, his hands tracing her body with lingering possession, and flames began to flicker all over her, the aching feeling inside growing so fast that she wound her arms round his neck and pulled him even closer.

'I've got to go,' he groaned, but his lips still probed hers deeply, his tongue searching the sweet darkness of her mouth, and Lauren's hands plucked frantically at his tie, pulling it free, tearing at the buttons of his shirt. 'Laurie, darling! I've got to go,' he said raggedly but her hands slid inside his shirt, caressing his skin, her lips planting wild kisses on his face and neck when he drew his head back. 'I want you with me,' he muttered unevenly, 'but I wouldn't get a damned thing done.'

His hold on her tightened and demanding lips captured her breast as he bent his dark head and Lauren fell back against the pillows, taking him with her, clutching him to her until he impatiently pushed the whole sheet aside and turned her into his arms. She had a tremendous feeling of triumph but he held her tightly, not letting her tempt him further, and when her agitated breathing had slowed a little he looked down at her vibrantly.

'No,' he said thickly. 'Taking you with me is never going to be a good idea, not if I want the Landis Group to survive.' He ran his hand slowly over her quivering body. 'You'll stay here until I get back. I want you waiting for me.'

'Like a mistress?' She met his green-eyed gaze squarely, her cheeks flushed, her eyes wild.

'Like a slave,' he corrected threateningly. 'I've waited most of my life for you.'

'You don't own me.' Lauren looked up at him pertly, trying to goad him into making love to her, and she got that old enigmatic smile, his eyes telling her he knew exactly what she was about.

'I do,' he said softly, his hand capturing her face. 'Every day I intend to own you a little more.' He was suddenly serious, the smile dying. 'Think about me?' he asked with an almost wistful look.

'All the time. Every minute.' Tears came to her eyes and he bent to kiss them away.

'I'm not going to Mars,' he assured her with a laugh. He glanced at his watch and stood quickly, pulling the sheet over her and reaching for his tie. 'Get in touch with Jill later. I'm not sure how many you'll be catering for but I think about twelve. Oh, yes, and can you give them a bit of choice in case of any allergies, pet dislikes and so forth? I never thought to mention that before.'

He was tucking his shirt in and reaching for his jacket, back to normal so swiftly that the passion never seemed to have been there. Lauren was still watching him wide-eyed as he arrived at the door.

'You never think of anything but business,' she complained, and he turned to look at her with amusement.

'Oh, sure! That's why I'm not kissing you goodbye. Business is uppermost in my mind. If I can just hang on to that thought until I'm in the car I might just make it to the meeting. I'll be OK then. Jill will take my ticket and beat me about the ears with it if I try to slide out of the New York trip. I never knew just how much I needed a good, bossy secretary. Living with a witch has its problems.'

'Am I living with you?' Lauren asked quietly, and his eyes met hers across the room, the amusement dying. 'You want out?'

'No.' She shook her head frantically. 'I didn't mean that. You—you know I want to be with you.' She suddenly jumped out of bed and ran across to him, not caring that his eyes flared over her and dark colour stained his cheekbones. There was heated desire in his gaze but he didn't move towards her.

'Don't go!' She threw her arms round him and for a second he grasped her convulsively.

'Laurie, you're crazy,' he whispered. 'Do you think I would be going if I didn't have to? I'd rather spend the day moving your things into my room and having our meals served there.'

'I'm sorry. You—you make me do mad things,' she said distractedly, blushing at the look in his eyes. 'I— I'm all right with other people.'

'So am I,' he laughed. 'It must be our past.' He kissed her quickly and left and Lauren trailed back to bed, her skin still tingling, every nerve-ending attuned to him. The week would seem like a year. How had she managed for so long in her life without Ryan? She loved him so much that there was no room for anything else.

She did all her arranging with Jill. The meeting was for Thursday and this time Jill had the numbers right. Without Ryan there the whole thing took on the aspect of a real job and it cheered Lauren up somewhat. Before long there would be a whole spate of these lunches and if all went well she would be firmly established, very competent when Ryan wanted her to be more adventurous.

With Jane and Cynthia to supervise, the whole thing to arrange and Maria and Constanza to be taken with her, Lauren had to be very efficient and she enjoyed it. She loved striding into the building with her entourage behind her. She loved the feeling that she was part of Ryan's powerful world and when the young man at the door sprang out and took her car away with a cheerful, 'Morning, Miss Moore!' it just made her day.

Things went smoothly and she had the satisfaction of knowing that she could do a worthwhile job under pressure. Her small staff worked well together and it gave her time to supervise things in the dining-room. Ryan would have been pleased.

It all came back to that—what Ryan thought—and now she never even tried to deny it. He was everything to her. He made the world seem bright and wonderful. He had made it like that when she was a child and a very young teenager but now there was so much more. She admitted with joy that she belonged to him. She always would.

On Friday, Alice called to ask Lauren to go shopping with her and as she had nothing specific to do but simply wait for Ryan she was happy to agree. He had not called and she was still filled with doubts and worries. It would pass one more day and maybe he would be back by the weekend.

Shopping proved to be interesting and quite exhausting as Alice darted everywhere at high speed.

'I give in. You win,' Lauren said finally. 'You might have told me it was a race then I could have gone into training.'

'Nearly finished,' Alice laughed. 'You go across the road and get a coffee. I just have to bully my dressmaker for a minute and then I'll join you.'

She hurried off and Lauren shook her head in amusement before dodging across the road and going into the small bar with windows that looked on to the street. Alice was much more than a minute.

'Refill, honey?' The waitress hovered over Lauren with more coffee and Alice was still not there.

'Not yet, thanks.' Lauren smiled up at her but her smile died as as she looked over the waitress's shoulder. Janice Powers was walking in and making her way forward with every intention of sitting at the same table.

'I saw you from the street,' she informed Lauren, settling herself comfortably and ordering coffee in her usual imperious manner. 'All by yourself?'

'Actually no. Alice Sheldon is with me.' It was almost impossible to be even civil with this woman. The thought of her had been in Lauren's mind so often that she wanted to walk out and not look back. Janice Powers was close to Ryan—how close? Jealousy hit her again as it always did.

'Has she been detailed to look after you—keep you occupied?' Janice sat back and smiled in a very superior manner and Lauren's blood began to boil.

'We're friends,' she said shortly.

'Well, I suppose Ryan approves,' Janice mused spitefully. 'You have to have someone, of course, and you can't be seeing much of Ryan.'

'He's away on business a lot,' Lauren managed tightly. 'I expected nothing else when he asked me to come to California with him.'

'I'm astonished he bothered to take you under his wing,' Janice said. 'Outside business hours he has a very full life—I should know, being part of it. You're going to be very bored finally.'

'I'm never bored,' Lauren assured her hotly. 'I work for Ryan in any case. I rather think that he'll be home much more now.'

'Don't bank on it, dear.' Janice began to gather her things. 'I'll have to rush. I'm flying out to New York tonight. You do know that Ryan is there, I suppose?'

'Yes, I know,' Lauren said, fighting down misery. 'He may be back this weekend.'

'Oh, he won't,' Janice assured her firmly, looking quite surprised. 'I don't know where you got that idea from. I couldn't get away until now and he's hardly likely to come back here just as I arrive in New York, is he?'

She walked out briskly and Lauren stared down into her cold coffee, fighting back tears. She had known it. She had known it right from the first, so why was she so surprised, so devastated? Ryan had a long-standing relationship with that woman. Janice Powers was out of the same tough mould. She could talk business with him, help him, hold her own in the places he frequented.

Janice Powers was not a person who had drifted through life with no aim. She wouldn't do stupid things, act like an idiot. She didn't need to hide behind glamour like a shield, it was a natural part of her. Ryan would never have to tell Janice that she was crazy and she wouldn't beg him to stay when she knew he had important business meetings.

'What happened to you? Can't I leave you for even a minute without gloom setting in?'

Lauren looked up to see Alice hovering over her anxiously and she didn't need to wonder how her friend came to question her miserable expression. She knew how she must look and she was quite beyond subterfuge.

'I've just been talking to Janice Powers,' she confessed as Alice slid into the seat beside her.

'Oh! Why did I leave you? I don't know what she said, Lauren, but whatever it was she's lying.'

'I don't think so. She's just about to leave for New York. Ryan's there.'

'It's a big place.'

'Thanks, Alice, but it's no use. She's meeting him; she told me so. He won't be back this weekend now.'

CHAPTER TEN

'LISTEN! She's lying!' Alice said urgently after the waitress had served her with coffee and they could talk again. 'She saw you and she came in to upset you. I know her like a book.'

'Ryan has never intimated that she was just a colleague,' Lauren whispered. 'He—he seems to talk about her a lot.'

'You love him, don't you?' Alice surmised quietly.

'Of course I do! He—he practically brought me up. We—we were almost like family...'

'You don't have to pretend with me, honey,' Alice assured her softly. 'You're in love with Ryan and I'll never believe he's not in love with you.'

'Janice knows differently,' Lauren muttered dismally, but Alice snorted under her breath.

'There are words for people like Janice Powers but I'll not assault your English ears with them. Anyway, you're not sitting miserably waiting for Ryan. You're coming with us this weekend.'

'I—I don't want you bothering with all this,' Lauren began but Alice looked at her triumphantly.

'The boss asked Jim to keep an eye on you,' she pronounced. 'What about that, then? He cares all right.'

'It's only what Janice said,' Lauren told her. 'She said Ryan would want somebody to entertain me as he would have his own things to do—that being taking her out.'

Alice swore in a very unladylike manner and drew Lauren to her feet.

'Janice Powers knows nothing,' she said angrily. 'All her talk about Ryan is wishful thinking. The other night, Ryan never took his eyes from you. You're crazy.'

'That's what Ryan says,' Lauren muttered unhappily. 'I suppose I am too. Why should Ryan change his life for me?'

'I will not have this morbid conversation!' Alice announced forcefully. 'You will go to the beach house, pack a bag and return with me forthwith!'

There was no stopping her and Lauren was not in any state to hold her own against Alice's forceful character. She found herself being driven away from the beach house with clothes for the weekend and a promise of sun, air and wine. It would take more than that to cheer her up. She couldn't think further than the next miserable minute.

Alice and Jim had a house further up the coast but unlike Ryan's house it was set into the hill, the sea still visible but not so dramatically close. Lauren felt at home immediately and as she sat with Alice on the veranda that evening, looking out over the lights of other houses towards the sea, she was glad she had come.

'Things will sort themselves out,' Alice said quietly. She had been unusually silent for a while and Lauren knew she was still thinking the situation over.

'I expect they will,' Lauren agreed. She didn't really want to talk about it. From delirious happiness she was sunk into near-despair and no amount of sympathy would help.

'What will you do in the meantime?' It was something that Lauren had tried not to decide. It all depended on Ryan. He might come back with a new attitude. He might want to just carry on as normal. On the other hand he cared about her and she had no doubts about that. She also knew she could never share him.

'I'm here to work. I've got a job. I intend to go on doing it.' That was something she had thought about too. There would be no running, no sliding back into her old attitude. For one thing she was now another person and for another she would never be able to face her old sort of life again. 'I'll behave like an employee, like Jim and Shaw. I'll take a flat in the city or something.'

'You imagine Ryan will let you escape?' Alice scoffed. 'I don't know why I started this lunatic conversation. When Ryan gets back you're going to find out that Janice Powers is lying—and don't forget I told you so either.'

'I'll remember,' Lauren promised, forcing a laugh. 'Let's not talk about it. What are we going to do tomorrow?'

'Sit on the boat, swim, eat and generally waste our time,' Alice announced. 'We'll not sail anywhere. We'll just hang around. Jim will fish. I've got it all planned.'

She had not planned on Shaw arriving, though; that was clear when he drove up the next day as they were on the boat. His car, a white convertible, drew up along the quayside and he got out with a rueful but cheery look at Lauren.

'I know,' he agreed, smiling apologetically. 'Safer is a long way off but what the hell? I like you, Lauren.'

'I like you too. Did anyone tell you differently?' She stood on the deck smiling down at him and he looked greatly relieved not to have been given his marching orders.

'Well, Ryan...'

'Oh, get on board!' Alice shouted. 'We're not going anywhere and you can help with the meals. Lauren is not cooking. I absolutely forbid it.'

It was all the invitation he wanted and Lauren was pleased to see him. He was good company and she doubted he would try anything amorous from now on. He was cautious and he had felt Ryan's displeasure. It made things safe at any rate.

The morning passed lazily. Alice liked pottering about on the boat and Jim hardly spoke. He was happily fishing from the dinghy. They could see him each time they looked up. He came in for lunch and then prepared to go out again.

'Watch the sea,' Alice ordered worriedly. 'There's a swell running.'

'Hmm. Want me to give it a miss?' Jim asked.

'I'd be glad,' Alice confessed, hugging him, and he readily settled down to read on board.

Shaw was not so happy. At the mention of a swell running he went to the side of the boat to scan the sea.

'Surf,' he told Lauren with more excitement than she had ever seen him possess. 'We get some good runs along here. Want to try it? I've got my gear in the car.'

'I've never surfed in my life,' Lauren told him with a smile, but he shrugged and dismissed her caution.

'Nothing to it. I'm not suggesting you stand up and give us a show. You can come in on the board lying flat. It's great fun.'

'Oh, I don't know, Lauren,' Alice said a little anxiously.

Jim too added words of warning. 'You can pick up speeds along here that take some handling,' he murmured.

'It's only just starting!' Shaw protested, but Jim shook his head.

'You know as well as I do that a heavy breaker can come unexpectedly.'

All this fatherly advice had Lauren remembering how she had always just given in to Ryan. She had never been adventurous. This was a new life. Why not acquire a new skill?

'I'll just make a gentle try at it,' she promised and in spite of Jim's frowning disapproval and Alice's worried looks she went. 'Just ten minutes,' she said, glancing back as she left the boat. She didn't like to worry people but she was old enough to take her chances after all. It might take her mind off Ryan.

It turned out to be fun. Shaw had all the necessary equipment and was something of an expert but he did not urge Lauren to try anything spectacular.

'Just get the feel of the waves,' he ordered, handing her a large, flat board. 'Walk out, wait for a breaker and float in on it. It picks up speed and that will be all you can handle at first.'

'Don't worry,' Lauren assured him, 'I'm not going to try and match you.' She had already watched him swim out with his board and come skimming in on the crest of a quite large wave but she was not at all deceived into thinking it was easy.

She waded out and made no attempt to go further than shoulder-deep, Shaw keeping at the side of her. They waited, watching the swell and seeing a white-topped wave gather momentum.

'OK!' Shaw yelled. 'Turn to face the beach but keep an eye on the lead wave. When it hits you jump with it and get flat down on the board.'

It was easy, exhilarating and the board skimmed to the shore, gathering speed and making Lauren scream with excitement. It tossed her off unceremoniously as she hit the sand and pebbles and she staggered to her feet, gasping and laughing as Shaw grabbed her arm.

'Fantastic! Let's do it again!' For those few seconds her mind had completely left Ryan and she wanted to go back to that state. It suited Shaw and her lessons progressed rapidly until after several spectacular and speedy rides he pronounced her grounded.

'No more, Lauren,' he ordered, hauling her to her feet. 'It's getting a bit wild out there. You can sit here and watch me. I need a spot of admiration.' He led her up the beach with her board and then ran down to the water to catch the now thunderous surf.

Lauren turned to the boat; it was riding easily and safely, tied to the quay in a little haven of calm. She raised her hand, waving to Alice and Jim, smiling when they instantly relaxed and moved away from their anxious vigil by the side of the boat.

She felt as if she had known them for years and she knew it was not just because of Ryan that they had been worried. They liked her. She had made good friends; Shaw too was a friend. Her life in London had been too superficial to have real friends. In many ways, she had been superficial too. Life was very real now and very poignant, her love for Ryan filling each corner of her mind and heart.

She looked towards the quay at the sound of an engine and her face paled when she saw Ryan's sleek car nosing its way forward as he looked for the boat. He was back! He was looking for her. Normally she would have jumped up and run towards him but now she couldn't. Why was he back so soon? Janice had only just gone out to New York. Had they quarrelled? Had Ryan's loyalty forced him back?

She didn't want loyalty, affection, protection, the things he had always given her. She wanted love, all his love, and now she couldn't face him at all. She stood quickly and scooped up her board. In seconds he would see her and she was in no way composed enough to greet him. Sooner or later she must do, but not now, not when he had come so unexpectedly, the sight of him almost stopping her heart.

The car cruised along and she knew he would soon find where she was. In a minute he would call to her. She raced down the beach and waded into the sea, ignoring the way the swell had grown, totally discounting the deep white froth on the edge of the leading waves. She went further than she had done before, forgetting danger in her desire to hide from Ryan's all-seeing green eyes.

Shaw was riding in on a huge wave, his wet body balanced skilfully, and it was only then that she saw the enormous wave behind it, a mountainous wave that Shaw seemed to be trying to outrun. It reared up like a live thing, dark, sinuous and threatening, topped by wild white foam, coming towards her like a thunderbolt.

'Lauren! No! Go back!' Shaw spotted her even with his own position precarious and his voice alerted the people on the quay.

'My God!' Jim saw her first and his gasp of distress brought Ryan spinning round. He had only just left his car and had not even climbed on the boat. Now his eyes slashed across the water, homing in on Lauren, taking in the situation, his actions instantaneous.

Before anyone could move he was running to the water's edge, shrugging out of his jacket and tie as he ran, discarding his shoes, and even before the wave hit Lauren Ryan was swimming out, taking the waves diagonally, his head dark and sleek with water as he made his way towards her.

Lauren didn't know. She was almost transfixed with fear. Shaw discarded his board, leaping into the waves to try and reach her, but the giant wave caught her, tossing her like a leaf, tearing her board from her grasp and hurtling her towards the beach as if she were nothing more than a doll.

Water choked her. There was not even time for real panic. She was spun round, submerged, flung up again and propelled forward helplessly. It was impossible to breathe and all fight was useless. As she neared the beach she was dragged along the bottom, scraping on sharp sand, overpowered by wild water, her arms and legs wrenched in all directions.

Something hit her head. It was hard, blinding, a red haze dimming her eyes and then blackness surged upwards to engulf her.

How stupid! How ridiculous! Her mind seemed to be holding its own assessment even as she plunged into darkness. She was caught, held fast, arms like iron lashing round her. 'Ryan!' She choked his name, knowing the feel of those arms even in her state of weakness, and then she fell into the black abyss, a dead weight, her fair hair hanging over his arm, its dazzling beauty blackened by water, her forehead already darkening from the bruising contact with a rock.

'They're keeping you overnight.' When Lauren came round, Alice was sitting by the bed, holding her hand. 'You're all right but you took in a lot of water and they want to see that the head is in good shape.'

'Ryan?' Lauren winced as she moved her head. Her face was white, the dark bruise startling against her pallor and the silver-gilt gleam of her hair.

'He got you out,' Alice said slowly, glancing at her. 'You were running away from him and he knows it. I don't know what possessed you, Lauren. I've never seen Ryan look like that, so stark, bitter. His eyes just didn't seem to see anything. He looked as if he wasn't there at all when we brought you both into the hospital.'

'Ryan's here?' Lauren tried to sit up but sank back with a low moan as pain shot through her head. 'Why? What's wrong with him? Where is he?'

'He needed a couple of stitches. He's not here now anyway. He went home.'

'He—he went without seeing me?' Lauren whispered, shaken by the news, her dark eyes distressed.

'He was angry,' Alice explained, patting her hand comfortingly. 'I imagine he thought he would be better with just his own company. Shaw got off lightly as it turned out because he tried to get to you and Ryan was too busy getting you out to take Shaw apart. I think the thought was there, though.'

When Alice left it was already getting dark and Lauren lay back exhausted. She had been idiotic as usual. There was no way she could have run away from Ryan. All she had done was cause trouble. She had risked not only her own life but Ryan's too, Shaw's also in all probability. Now wonder Ryan needed a sophisticated, mature woman around him. Now she had made herself appear more foolish than ever.

He couldn't even face seeing her and she knew why. Now he would have to make some other arrangement and he was not going to tell her when she was in this state. He wouldn't have to tell her. She would take action herself, let him out of the embarrassing situation by simply leaving. It would have to be London too. As long as she was here she was Ryan's responsibility, however much she denied it.

Ryan never came. Next morning she was feeling better, her headache down to bearable proportions. It was Sunday and he would not be at work. He could have come but he had not. When the time went on and he still stayed away, she decided to leave and no one could stop her. She dressed and called a cab. Dreading things was much worse than facing them. She had to set Ryan's mind at rest.

The beach house was empty, the veranda doors wide open. Today the girls took their day off and invariably went out but there was no sign of Ryan either and the open doors were worrying. She searched the house but she could find no clue as to where he was. Finally she went to her room and changed, getting into bed because the trip had tired her more than she had expected.

Lauren was almost asleep when she heard a noise in the house. Whoever it was there was no attempt at a quiet entrance and she knew it could only be Ryan. Of course, he had no idea she was home.

She grimaced as the word came to her mind. Home! Soon this would not be home and it had come to mean everything to her, being here with Ryan. Being with him had always meant everything to her but now she would have to leave, now there would be no future because after this it would not be the Ryan she had known.

Now she loved him differently and so much more. It was something she had to do all the same and she slid quietly from the bed, putting on her wrap and making her way to the big room that faced the sea. Afternoon sunlight flooded in and for a moment she didn't see him at all. When she did, she was shocked at how pale and weary he looked.

He was sitting with his knees apart, his arms hanging loosely, his head bent. His dark hair was untidy as if he had been walking in the wind for hours and he looked tired enough to have done just that. He was miles away, lost in his own thoughts, and she could tell that his thoughts were not at all happy ones.

It didn't need a lot of thinking out. Ryan was torn between two worlds, the past when he had cared for her all the time and now when he had made love to her and destroyed the old relationship forever. He needed Janice but he had bound himself to his stepsister with no going back.

Even though tears threatened, Lauren found it possible to feel at least some sort of happiness. Now at last she could do something for Ryan. She could persuade him that it didn't matter, that she would be glad to leave. It would straighten everything out and leave him in peace.

'Ryan?' She said his name softly and his head shot up, his eyes vividly green as he saw her standing there.

'How did you get here?' he asked roughly. 'Why did they let you out of hospital? Nobody told me.'

'I left of my own accord. I'm perfectly all right and saw no reason to stay there longer. I have a lot of things to do.'

'Like what?' He stood slowly, never taking his eyes from her. 'Don't tell me you've arranged to meet

Newark? I'm not sure he's recovered yet anyway. He doesn't seem to be as tough as you.'

'I expect you were angry with him,' Lauren began, 'but really it was my own stupid fault because——'

'There's no need at all to defend him,' Ryan interrupted harshly. 'I didn't attempt to kill him, I'm not about to get rid of him and he did his best to get you out. Still, I suppose he's told you that already?'

'Alice told me. I haven't seen Shaw. I—I've only seen Alice. She—she said you were hurt. I'm sorry I...'

'Save your sympathy, Lauren,' he grated. 'A couple of stitches isn't going to bother me for long. Injuries are the least of my problems.'

He turned away, staring out to sea, and Lauren bit into her lip anxiously. It wasn't going to be easy. She had to be firm and businesslike, no tears, no sign of any misery or Ryan would sacrifice everything for her as he had always been prepared to do.

'I've decided to go back to England,' she told him, keeping her voice carefully controlled. 'I—I don't think this is going to work out after all. You have a life of your own and clearly I'm just complicating things. It would be better all round if I went back to London.'

'To Redmond? Or do you have other plans?' He spun round and stared at her bitterly. 'I suppose I shouldn't be too startled. Drifting from one thing to another has become a way of life with you, hasn't it?'

'It probably has,' Lauren agreed quietly. His attitude was not quite what she had expected but she knew he was feeling guilty and she was prepared to let any harsh words just hit her without retaliation. 'I'm not going because of that, though. I meant what I just said. I can't go on complicating your life.'

'Don't you think you've already complicated it?' he snapped. He took a step towards her and he looked so furious, so odd that she felt a wave of faintness wash over her. The weakness she thought she had conquered came sweeping back and she swayed dizzily.

'You're not fit to be out of hospital!' He strode towards her angrily, making her begin to back away. 'Can't you ever do what you're supposed to do? Am I never going to be able to leave you without worrying?'

'I'm capable of living my own life without assistance,' Lauren said weakly, a little cry of sheer panic leaving her lips as he suddenly swept her into his arms and strode off towards her room.

'You're not even capable of thinking straight,' he growled angrily, shouldering his way into her room and making for the bed determinedly. 'You should be resting and you know it but instead you're standing like a ghost, telling me all sorts of nonsense that you know I'll ignore.'

He put her on the bed and Lauren looked up at him wildly. She was trying to help him, willing to sacrifice her own life for him, and he wouldn't even listen. She could feel anger mounting inside her in spite of her determination to play this quietly and calmly.

'You have no control over me! I've told you what I intend to do.' He just stared down at her and she became more annoyed by the second. Apparently he was not about to even speak. 'Are you listening to me?' she demanded crossly. 'Do you understand what I'm saying? Answer yes or no. Please tick appropriate box!'

'I'm listening,' he said darkly. 'I understand fully. You're running out on us.' He sighed and turned away. 'I'm funny about you, Lauren. I've spent most of the day just wandering about on the beach, coming to conclusions. I decided quite calmly to let you go. I worked it all out logically. You're young, you're used to another sort of life, I have a long-time hold on you that I've shamelessly exploited. I'm aware how much of a hero I've always been to you. Your hero turned out to be a villain, though. He made love to you, bound you to him and didn't leave you much choice at all.' He shrugged and walked across to the window, staring out. 'I thought it all out, you see. I decided to let you go, help you to go, let you make your choices even though, belatedly, I figured you were young enough to survive from having a first lover.'

She was disappointed in him. It would have been more in his character to tell her straight out about Janice but she set her lips and let him have it this way if he wanted.

'So we're in complete agreement,' she managed quietly. 'You think I should go. I want to go.'

'Oh, I worked it all out,' he murmured, turning towards her again. 'The trouble is, I'm funny about you, as I told you. The moment I looked up and saw you my logical conclusions went out of the window.' He watched her with a wry, self-deprecating look on his face. 'If you leave, I'll just follow you,' he finished quietly.

'But why?' His words had sent a shock right through her. It was impossible not to hope but she knew him so well. He was doing it again, giving things up for her. 'It's all right, Ryan,' she got out desperately. 'I understand. I know all about Janice.'

'Do you?' He began to walk back to her and she saw that quirk to his lips that she knew so well. 'What do you know about Janice? Something Alice told you? Is it scandalous? Alice usually knows some juicy bits of scandal. But about Janice? I'm intrigued. Do tell me.'

'Please, Ryan, don't joke,' she begged almost tearfully, and he sat beside her on the bed, watching her in amusement.

'Who's joking? You think men don't like to gossip? What do you know about Janice?'

'I know you're lovers.' She hung her head to hide tears. 'I know she was in New York with you for at least some of the time. I—I realise that she's what you need. You—you've always been my friend, Ryan,' she whispered distractedly. 'You've listened to my miseries, kept my secrets, loved me all my life like a friend...' She had to stop because tears were filling her eyes and soon they would be in her voice.

Ryan never attempted to touch her but he was deeply silent for a minute and she knew she had finally got through to him.

'Do you love me, Laurie?' he asked softly and she looked up then, tears on her cheeks, her eyes unable to deceive him. He just held her glance, his own eyes softening to dark green, deep as the sea, changing and wonderful. 'Yes,' he murmured. 'I've loved you all your life. I had very little choice because you were a sort of magic to me. You're not a baby now, though, not a little girl. I've wanted you since you were seventeen. That was when I realised that my beautiful Laurie was growing up fast. That was was when I got scared that somebody would take you from me.'

'I—I don't know what you're saying,' Lauren whispered in a choked voice and he gathered her into his arms, cradling her against him, smiling down at her.

'You do. I want you with me always. I'll never let anyone take you from me. Oh, I'm your friend, my sweet Laurie, but I'm your lover too and I want to be a whole lot more. I never want to let you out of my sight. I want to marry you as soon as possible.'

'Marry me?' She stared up at him dazedly, her eyes filling with tears again. 'I didn't want to leave you,' she wept. 'I love you, Ryan.'

'I know,' he murmured, kissing her tears away.

'I—I don't love you the way I used to...'

'I'm glad about that,' he assured her tenderly, 'because I love you differently too. Are you going to stop trying to order me about? Are you going to marry me?' She just nodded her head, biting at her lips to try and stop the foolish tears that were turning to tears of happiness, and he stroked back her fair hair, his eyes on her trembling mouth. 'Laurie,' he said gently. 'My burden, my darling, my life.'

Lauren buried her head against his shoulder when at last his lips released hers. Her arms wound tightly around his neck as he rocked her against him and she muttered her worries.

'What about Janice?'

'Janice is very smooth,' Ryan assured her comfortably. 'She's quite an admirable female, you know.' When Lauren's head shot up and her eyes flashed sparks she found he was grinning down at her. 'Janice does have a fault, though,' he admitted, laughing into her dark eyes. 'She tells very slick lies. I'm surprised Alice didn't acquaint you with that fact.'

'She did,' Lauren said, flushing with embarrassment.

'You should listen to her,' Ryan suggested. 'Alice may have the habit of saying things that people don't really want to hear but she's a quite extraordinary gossip and never deviates from the truth.' He bent his dark head to kiss her and then looked seriously into her eyes. 'Janice Powers plays a never-ending game of romance and intrigue, but never with me. I've been hooked for a long, long time. I belong to you.'

His kisses were warm and loving but after a minute Lauren twisted against him as heat began to spread through her limbs.

'Does it hurt?' she asked seriously, her fingers delicately touching the dressing on his arm where he had been stitched.

'Not now,' he said huskily. 'If you weren't still weak I would take that as an invitation.'

'I'm not weak,' Lauren assured him earnestly and then blushed rosy pink at the way he laughed. 'I was going to give you up,' she said with a pained glance at him.

'For Janice? What sort of friendship is that?' he teased. He was suddenly serious, stroking her face gently. 'If she ever says anything again you'll know what to do.'

'I will!' Lauren assured him fiercely, remembering her own misery when she should have been so happy after that wonderful night with Ryan.

'You'll dangle your wedding-ring under her nose and laugh in her face,' he cautioned. 'I don't want her maimed. She's too damned good at her job.'

'If she's going to flirt with my husband...'

'She doesn't dare,' Ryan laughed. 'She's a career woman and I have a reputation for being quite nasty when necessary.'

'I could be a career woman,' Lauren mused, but Ryan looked at her sceptically, his hands carefully undressing her.

'How many jobs do you want?' he murmured thickly. 'Cordon bleu caterer, friend, wife, mother. That's enough to be going on with.' And Lauren smiled shyly at the look in his eyes. She couldn't find anything wrong with that list of jobs.

Later, as she lay in his arms, her whole being softened with love, Ryan smiled down at her tenderly.

'All our lives we've been heading towards this. Nobody could possibly belong together as much as we do, darling,' he whispered.

'I must have been very stupid not to know it,' Lauren admitted softly, touching his face with loving fingers. 'Nothing was ever quite right,' she sighed. 'Without you there was emptiness in everything.'

'So why were you going back?' he asked quietly. 'Were you giving me up without a fight?'

'I thought it was best for you. I wanted to give you something without any selfishness.'

'Luckily I know you very well,' he pointed out, and she smiled sweetly at him.

'I love you so much, Ryan. I wanted you to be happy.'

'Without you? How could I be? I never have been happy away from you. I was just waiting for you to grow up. You can imagine how I felt when Sylvia wrote to tell me you were getting engaged.'

'You came back to stop me,' Lauren reminded him smugly.

'I did. Even then I wasn't sure if I could stop you, or even if I had the right.' He suddenly gripped her chin fiercely. 'You asked me to give you away,' he growled. 'My God! It nearly killed me just to think about it.'

'I would have run away,' Lauren said urgently, holding him tightly when he looked grief-stricken at the very thought of losing her. 'I would have run back to you.'

'You'd better wipe that phrase from your vocabulary,' Ryan threatened. 'Running away is something that will never be allowed.'

'Why should I run away when I'm right where I want to be?' Lauren asked softly. 'I'm in love for the first time and the last time. I couldn't live without you for one single minute.'

'Then we've finally arrived,' he said huskily. 'The end of a wonderful journey with another one before us but this time we'll know where we're going. This time we travel together.'

Accept 4 FREE Romances and 2 FREE gifts

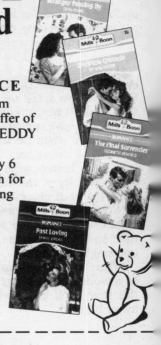

FROM READER SERVICE

Here's an irresistible invitation from Mills & Boon. Please accept our offer of 4 FREE Romances, a CUDDLY TEDDY and a special MYSTERY GIFT! Then, if you choose, go on to enjoy 6 captivating Romances every month for just £1.80 each, postage and packing FREE. Plus our FREE Newsletter with author news, competitions and much more.

Send the coupon below to: Mills & Boon Reader Service, FREEPOST, PO Box 236, Croydon, Surrey CR9 9EL.

— ▪ NO STAMP REQUIRED ▪ —

Yes! Please rush me 4 FREE Romances and 2 FREE gifts! Please also reserve me a Reader Service subscription. If I decide to subscribe I can look forward to receiving 6 brand new Romances for just £10.80 each month, post and packing FREE. If I decide not to subscribe I shall write to you within 10 days - I can keep the free books and gifts whatever I choose. I may cancel or suspend m subscription at any time. I am over 18 years of age.

Ms/Mrs/Miss/Mr _____ EP55I

Address _____

_____

Postcode _____ Signature _____

Next Month's Romances

Each month you can choose from a wide variety of romance with Mills & Boon. Below are the new titles to look out for next month, why not ask either Mills & Boon Reader Service or your Newsagent to reserve you a copy of the titles you want to buy – just tick the titles you would like and either post to Reader Service or take it to any Newsagent and ask them to order your books.

Please save me the following titles:	Please tick	√
UNWILLING MISTRESS	Lindsay Armstrong	
DARK HERITAGE	Emma Darcy	
WOUNDS OF PASSION	Charlotte Lamb	
LOST IN LOVE	Michelle Reid	
ORIGINAL SIN	Rosalie Ash	
SUDDEN FIRE	Elizabeth Oldfield	
THE BRIDE OF SANTA BARBARA	Angela Devine	
ISLAND OF SHELLS	Grace Green	
LOVE'S REVENGE	Mary Lyons	
MAKING MAGIC	Karen van der Zee	
OASIS OF THE HEART	Jessica Hart	
BUILD A DREAM	Quinn Wilder	
A BRIDE TO LOVE	Barbara McMahon	
A MAN CALLED TRAVERS	Brittany Young	
A CHILD CALLED MATTHEW	Sara Grant	
DANCE OF SEDUCTION	Vanessa Grant	

If you would like to order these books in addition to your regular subscription from Mills & Boon Reader Service please send £1.80 per title to: Mills & Boon Reader Service, Freepost, P.O. Box 236, Croydon, Surrey, CR9 9EL, quote your Subscriber No:.................................. (If applicable) and complete the name and address details below. Alternatively, these books are available from many local Newsagents including W.H.Smith, J.Menzies, Martins and other paperback stockists from 14 January 1994.

Name:..

Address:...

....Post Code:.........................

To Retailer: If you would like to stock M&B books please contact your regular book/magazine wholesaler for details.

You may be mailed with offers from other reputable companies as a result of this application. If you would rather not take advantage of these opportunities please tick box ☐